"I had this idea, Madelyn."

He's going to ask me to move in with him, she was thinking, and she knew she was beginning to look excited. "What is it?" she asked, trying to keep the interest out of her voice.

"I think I've figured out a way we can be together."

She didn't know why it had taken Eddie so long. She had figured it out days ago. "Tell me."

"I don't have to work as a building superintendent, you know."

You can be a super and I'll move in with you, she wanted to say, but she kept that silent. He seemed to be waiting for her to say something, so she said, "What're you getting at, Eddie?"

"Now don't hit the ceiling, Madelyn."

"I'm going to hit you if you don't get to the point pretty quick."

"I was thinking we could rob a bank."

ABOUT THE AUTHOR

Beverly Sommers likes living alone, traveling alone, neon palm trees and red furniture.

Books by Beverly Sommers

HARLEQUIN AMERICAN ROMANCE

HARLEQUIN INTRIGUE

HARLEQUIN AMERICAN ROMANCE
PREMIER EDITION

These books may be available at your local bookseller.

Don't miss any of our special offers. Write to us at the following address for information on our newest releases.

Harlequin Reader Service
P.O. Box 52040, Phoenix, AZ 85072-2040
Canadian address: P.O. Box 2800, Postal Station A, 5170 Yonge St., Willowdale, Ont M2N 6J3

Convictions
BEVERLY SOMMERS

Harlequin Books

TORONTO • NEW YORK • LONDON
AMSTERDAM • PARIS • SYDNEY • HAMBURG
STOCKHOLM • ATHENS • TOKYO • MILAN

Published February 1986

First printing December 1985

ISBN 0-373-16137-9

Chapter One

It's odd how the least expected things always happen
while carrying the sense that they have been expected
all along.

Madelyn was watering the six potted plants that sat
on the sills of her two windows when the buzzer to her
apartment sounded. She tipped up the spout of the
watering can and wondered who it could be. Because
it was still before noon, and no one ever visited her in
the morning, she deduced it was the mail carrier with
something too large to be fitted into her mailbox in the
entry hall. And that something could only be the latest selection from the book club to which she sub-
scribed. She remembered now it had been a book on
exercising to keep fit, an oversized book filled with
pictures of skinny people trying to get even skinnier.
No, wait—a Jane Fonda book—yes, that was it. She
recalled thinking she would enjoy looking at the pictures of Jane Fonda even if she didn't care to exercise.

Except that once having expended the money on the
book she would now feel compelled to put into prac-

tice that which she had only thought about previously. For that matter, she wasn't sure her apartment afforded enough floor space to allow her to exercise.

The buzzer sounded again and she put down the watering can on the floor and went over and pushed the button that would release the door between the entry hall and the stairs; then she waited by the door for the book to be delivered. While she waited, she again wondered if she really had the space to exercise. Or even the inclination. She very often enjoyed reading about things she wouldn't actually want to do. There had been that book on scuba diving she had found on the dollar table at Barnes & Noble, and the needlepoint book that had been a Christmas gift from her grandmother—although she had enjoyed the pictures in that one....

The knock at the door interrupted her reverie and she realized she had forgotten what she had been waiting for. She looked through the peephole but didn't recognize the man as her regular mail carrier. Still, it was nearing Christmas and there were often extra people hired by the post office this time of year. Then again, it was New York and she had an inbred paranoia about opening the door to strangers. She finally unlocked two of the locks, and leaving the chain on the door, opened it and peered out.

It was definitely not the mail carrier. Not unless they had taken to carrying athletic bags rather than mail bags. "Yes?" she said, not even thinking beyond the fact that he must have the wrong apartment.

"Madelyn Shaffer?" He made it sound half question and half statement.

"Yes."

"It's me, Eddie Mello." He sounded tentative, as if he weren't quite sure.

It still hadn't quite registered; it was too out of context, for one thing. Eddie Mello wasn't a name she associated with a man standing at her door. But then he said, "Your pen pal?" and she was suddenly too stunned even to breathe.

This is what it feels like to have a heart attack, she couldn't help thinking, feeling the constriction in her chest and the chills running down her body, which had nothing to do with the cold air rushing in through the open door.

"Look," he said, "I know this is a shock...."

Without even thinking about it, her arms just taking over, she pushed the door shut and pressed all of her body weight against it, then felt the pent-up breath escaping from her mouth. This just wasn't something that could really be happening. It must be a joke, a joke perpetrated by Eddie. And yet she wouldn't have thought it of him.

She heard his voice quite clearly through the wood. "I'm sorry if I frightened you; I didn't mean to. I guess you don't like surprises."

He was right, she didn't like surprises. She liked jokes even less. And yet, what if it weren't a joke? What if the impossible had become actuality? She moved her mouth against the door. "How do I know you're really Eddie Mello?"

There was a silence; then he said, "If you could open the door again for a second—with the chain on, of course."

He sounded very polite, very reasonable. And if it really was Eddie Mello, she owed him that. After three years she could hardly deny him that. She opened the door again, and with a slow movement he pushed through a stack of envelopes with a piece of string tied around them. She saw that the skin on the back of his hand was as white as the paper.

She took the package in her hand and saw how worn the paper was. Thin, as though handled countless times. She recognized her handwriting and wondered what she was going to do. Then, knowing there wasn't anything else she could do, she closed the door, unfastened the chain and opened the door halfway.

Madelyn stared at the man she had been corresponding with for the past three years. In those three years she had pictured him a thousand different ways; finally, in just the past year, settling on tall, lean, with sandy-colored hair, gray eyes and, now that she thought of it, a close resemblance to Clint Eastwood. This idea was no doubt gleaned from some late-night movie on TV.

In actuality he was nothing like Clint Eastwood. He was of medium height and probably lean beneath his baggy coat, but his hair was dark and straight and his eyes a deep blue. He looked rather like Al Pacino might look if he weren't Italian. She liked the fact that he was clean-shaven: beards and mustaches proliferated in her neighborhood to the point where they lost any appeal they might have once had.

"This is really a shock to you, isn't it?" Eddie was saying, still standing there, looking lost and uncertain.

And because he looked the way she was feeling, Madelyn knew she was the one who must take the initiative. She stood aside. "Come in," she said, and when he still hesitated, she smiled. "You didn't tell me; I had no idea you were being released."

Immediately the thought that maybe he hadn't been released crossed her mind, and he must have seen it on her face because he quickly said, "Don't worry, I was released. I even took the extra three months so I wouldn't have to be on parole. Listen, I got my papers if you want to see them."

She tried to smile again but couldn't quite manage it. "No, that's all right; I believe you."

Eddie walked past her into the room and just stood there, immobile. He looked somehow out of date, or maybe out of place. For one thing, his hair was too short; and the terrible overcoat he was wearing hung down to the tops of his shoes. He could have been one of the men in the streets who occasionally asked her for money, even to the lack of any expression on his face. Then she noticed how very cold he looked and, remembering her manners, she said, "Would you care for a cup of hot coffee?"

His eyes met hers briefly before they both looked away. "What I'd really die for is a cold beer," he said, still holding on to the handle of his suitcase, a shabby affair of fake leather.

"I don't have any beer but I could run down to—" She broke off when she realized that would mean leaving him alone in her apartment. Then she felt instant remorse that she could even think such a thing. This man had been her friend and confidant for three years; surely she could trust him not to run off with her television set.

Yet for all she knew he could have been in prison for that very thing. During the three years they had corresponded she had never asked him why he had been incarcerated. At first she had felt it rude to ask; then, as time passed and he never volunteered the information himself, she felt she had left it too late. Except now he was standing in her apartment and she was alone with him, and for all she knew he could have been in for rape or murder.

"No, I wouldn't want you to do that. A glass of water would be fine."

His understanding left her feeling ashamed. Never, not in even one of his letters, had he ever given her cause to mistrust him. Of course, writing letters was so very safe. She saw that he was as uncomfortable with the situation as she was, was becoming unnerved by her silences. He had thought of her as a friend and had come to see her, and she was making him feel like some kind of criminal.

"How long has it been since you've had a beer, Eddie?"

A corner of his mouth lifted in the specter of a smile. "Ten years. And then I wasn't even old enough to be drinking it legally. Not in Jersey, anyway."

"Eddie?"

He just stood there looking at her.

Madelyn had fantasized this moment more times than she cared to admit even to herself, and now that it was really happening, she didn't even know how to talk to him. She tried to think of an appropriate line from a movie, but none came to mind.

She looked past him to the plants on the windowsills. "I would be honored to be the one to buy you your first beer in ten years." Even if it was still morning. And then, to show him he had her trust, she took her coat off the hook next to the front door, checked her pocket for her wallet, and said, "Put down that suitcase and make yourself at home. I'll just be a minute." But even as she said it she wondered if she should have told him to make himself at home.

"Madelyn?" The word a mere breath.

"Yes?"

Eddie shook his head. "Nothing. Maybe I'll write you a letter while you're gone."

She felt herself nodding, understanding what he meant. It was so much easier to communicate at a distance.

THE SOUND OF THE DOOR slamming behind her was jarring. Eddie supposed that it would be a long time before the sound of a door slamming shut ceased to affect him. And now that it was shut he realized something; he realized he felt more secure with it shut. The open door had given him a feeling of unease.

But then nearly everything that day had given him a feeling of unease. The worst had been the way things and people on the outside moved so fast. Cars. Pedestrians. Bicycles. A jogger in Madelyn's neighborhood had raced by him and he had found himself backing into the wall of a building and then looking around quickly, waiting for a guard to appear.

He stood where he was and turned around slowly, savoring the size of her apartment, its contents. It wasn't a large place; in fact, he imagined it was quite small as apartments went. Four strides in either direction would put him against a wall, or a piece of furniture. There was a lot of furniture.

What he noticed first were the touches of color. Mostly browns with the walls in beige, but here and there he would spot a vivid color: on a book jacket, a record album, a can of tomato soup on the counter in the kitchen portion of the room, a yellow towel hanging from a knob beneath the kitchen sink. His eyes went back and forth to the touches of color, soaking them up. He hadn't realized while he was in prison that it lacked color, but now he found the realization startling.

His eyes followed a ladder up to a bed built beneath the ceiling. He liked the way the ceiling was so high. He stretched his hands up as high as they would reach and still he was nowhere near touching it.

He looked around the room again, feeling a sense of familiarity. He couldn't put his finger on what the place reminded him of but it wasn't at all the way he had pictured Madelyn living. There was a patterned rug on the floor and the furniture was all dark and oversized. The lamps looked like antiques and even the paintings on the walls, in heavy, carved gold frames, looked old. One was a scene of the outdoors somewhere and the other was of a vase of roses.

He thought it looked like an old lady's apartment. The only modern touches were a small TV set and a stereo. The only signs of life were the plants on the windowsills.

The apartment had the feeling of a nest. It had a cluttered warm aura to it and it made him feel safer than the bus had done or being outside.

He spotted the watering can on the floor and figured out that she had been watering her plants when he had arrived. He walked over to the plants and reached out a gentle finger to touch one of the leaves. The only greenery they ever saw in prison had been the tops of trees on the other side of the walls. It had been kind of an "in" joke there to wonder if the trees had trunks to them or whether they really were just tops.

He picked up the watering can and poured water into one of the pots, but he hadn't paid careful enough attention because it overflowed the dish beneath and made a puddle on the floor. He went over and got the towel he had seen, but when he began soaking up the water he saw he was dirtying the towel, and he quickly exchanged the bottom of his coat for the towel. He didn't care if the coat got dirty. It was what they had given him to wear when he was released, and he wanted to get rid of it as soon as possible, along with the rest of the clothes. He didn't even want that reminder of prison.

He could see it had been a mistake to come without warning her. He had planned it for months, every detail, and never once had he considered that he might be making a mistake. Being able to come here had been the determining factor when he had turned down the early release. Parole would have meant going through all kinds of red tape if he wanted to leave the state, even if New Jersey did border New York.

Gradually during the past three years, so slowly it took a while before he was even aware of it, she had become the entire focus of his life. He had been warned about this when he had first been sent up. He had been told not to focus his mind on anything outside of the prison itself; that doing so would eventually affect him mentally, maybe even drive him nuts. The prison had to become the whole world, the only reality. You didn't count off days or months or years. You just lived each day and didn't think about the next.

Like the beer. Right now he could be torturing himself trying to remember what a beer tasted like, how it would feel going down, whether it would go to his head. But that wasn't the way to do it. That wasn't the smart way. He would just put it from his mind, not even try to experience it until the experience itself was at hand.

It hadn't worked that way with Madelyn. From the moment he and several of the other prisoners had had their ads placed for them in the *Village Voice*, he had been aware of something new in his life. Expectancy. Expectancy can be a magical thing, especially when you're at a slow point in your life, and being in prison was more than a slow point. It was a dead standstill.

Eddie hadn't received even one letter in seven years, so the thought of just a couple of replies had been something to look forward to. When, instead, they kept coming in day after day until he had over forty, he hadn't known how to handle it all.

He had read through the letters carefully, over and over, trying to weed out the ones he wanted to answer. When he finally had it down to five potentials, he traded the ones he didn't want with other guys on the cell block for cigarettes or candy.

Madelyn's letter hadn't been the most interesting one. It had been tentative and polite, and he thought the main reason why it had ended up being chosen by him at all was because she wrote that she never got personal letters, either. Of the five women he replied to, she was the only one he wrote to more than three times. One of them never wrote back; the other three—and this was something he hadn't anticipated—seemed to get turned on by the idea of writing to a convict. It hadn't been his intention to turn women on. In fact, about the last thing he wanted to be reminded of in prison was sex. As soon as the drift of their letters became clear to him, he handed them over to one of his friends who liked writing those kinds of letters. And from then on most of his waking hours revolved around writing to Madelyn and waiting for her replies.

He had never asked her for a picture and she had never sent him one, and while at first it sometimes occurred to him to wonder what she looked like, after a while he had such a strong sense of her that what she looked like ceased to matter. He had found that people were never what they looked like, anyway. Nor did what they do interest him. He felt he only really got to know someone by knowing how the person thought, and he had come to know Madelyn's thoughts as well as he knew his own.

Eddie realized that right now, maybe five minutes after seeing her for the first time, he would be unable to give an accurate description of her if asked. He had got an impression of gentleness bordering on timidity, but he tempered this assessment with the fact that his arrival had been completely unexpected. Visually he had taken in her pale, almost translucent skin, the heavy hair that had partially obscured her small face, the bulky clothes that gave her body a substantiality it might not possess.

The voice, though—that he would be able to describe. It was somewhat high, light, more the voice of a young girl than a grown woman.

He couldn't yet merge the person with the letters. It was as though they were separate entities, having no connection. He thought it would happen when they really started to talk. What had always amazed him about her letters was how she never ran out of subject matter. It had given him the feeling that if they were to meet, they would be able to talk for hours at a time without running out of anything to say.

It was more her doing than his. Eddie hadn't had much to write about before the correspondence began. He didn't want to write about his life because his life was so meaningless. And yet, even though she was on the outside, Madelyn didn't write about her life, either. Instead, she wrote about ideas and, in so doing, gave him new things to think about.

He figured she had to spend a lot of time reading because she often wrote about books she had read. At first he tended to skip those parts, but then one of the books she mentioned sounded interesting to him, and having plenty of spare time in prison, he visited the prison library to see if he could find the book. It turned out he couldn't, but while he was there he got another book to take back to his cell with him.

It was by some Russian writer she had once mentioned, and it was slow going at first, particularly when he tried to figure out the Russian names for the characters, but he kept at it and found that he liked reading better than staring at the walls. And then, at some point, he found he liked reading even better than watching television. Mostly because some of the guys never would shut up while they watched or else they argued continuously over which show to watch. At some point he switched from fiction to nonfiction and found that he could learn just about anything by reading a book about it. At that point you couldn't keep him away from books. They became the second most important things in his life; the first were Madelyn's letters.

He had been kidding around when he had told her maybe he'd write her a letter while she was out, but it might not be such a bad idea. He knew how to write to her; he wasn't sure he knew how to talk to her.

What he ought to do, what he felt like doing, was just walking out, finding a place to stay, then writing her a letter. She'd probably be real relieved if she came back and he was gone. Hell, on top of everything, she was probably scared of him. He had never actually told her what he was in for.

For all she knew, he might be some kind of maniac.

MADELYN DIDN'T KNOW where she had got the idea, but somehow she had been certain that Eddie was in prison for life. She didn't think she would have had the nerve to write to a prisoner if she thought there was a chance he was going to show up on her doorstep one day.

Often enough she had daydreamed about actually meeting him, but then she daydreamed about practically everything. This was the first time one of her dreams had ever come true. But that was the thing: daydreams weren't supposed to come true. They were supposed to remain just dreams—safe. As she thought writing to a prisoner would be.

Madelyn always read the *Village Voice* from cover to cover, and she would never have dreamed of answering one of the personal ads that appeared—ads put in by lonely New Yorkers who wanted to meet members of the opposite sex. She had also never considered answering one of the Pen Pal ads until she read Eddie's. It had been brief, merely saying that in seven years he had never received a letter.

She had read it twice, thinking how sad it would be if he still didn't receive a letter. Then, figuring that at least if she wrote him he would have received one, she wrote that first letter to him, keeping it friendly and impersonal. Then, of course, when he answered, she felt it would be rude not to reply in turn.

And it was fun getting his letters, a welcome change from junk mail and magazines.

Around his forty-seventh letter she fell in love with him. It wasn't real love. It was like falling in love with Ashley Wilkes when she saw *Gone With the Wind* for the first time or with Gabriel García Márquez when she read *One Hundred Years of Solitude*. She had a tendency to fall in love with men she didn't know. She had never fallen in love with a man she did know.

But the unexpected had happened. Her surprise at finding Eddie Mello—in person—at her door, was no less than it would have been had it been Ashley Wilkes standing there. Except Ashley Wilkes, being fictional, would have been easier to deal with.

The emotion she felt most strongly was a sense of loss. A great sense of loss that their correspondence was now at an end. She supposed that it was possible that they could continue writing to each other, but she had a feeling he wouldn't need it anymore. Now he was out of prison and could go about life as normal people do—meeting people in person, picking up the telephone, at the most sending a brief note. He wouldn't need her anymore.

That meant the most important part of her life would end. From the first short letters their correspondence had progressed to the point that she was writing him fifteen- to twenty-page handwritten letters, often spending hours on them. And no sooner did she receive one of his than she'd sit down to answer. Since the letters had only to go over the river to New Jersey, she often would write him twice a week and, sometimes, if she couldn't wait for his reply, she would write a third letter.

When she wasn't writing him she would reread the stacks of letters she had from him. She had one entire kitchen cupboard filled with his letters, filed under the month and the year they were written. Each time she reread them she would find new things to think about.

Clearly an obsession, she was thinking as she picked out a six-pack of beer and paid for it at the counter. But an obsession she was quite happy living with. An obsession she hated to see coming to an end.

It was the only thing she had had of her very own, the only thing she had never told anyone about. Why did he have to get out? Why couldn't he have stayed in prison forever and kept writing letters to her?

She knew that was a terrible thing to wish on him and she instantly regretted it. The poor man was finally free after what must have been ten very long years, and she was so selfish she was only thinking of her own pleasure.

She had one advantage. It was possible that she was the only person he knew in New York, his only friend there. And just maybe he would like her in person as well as he liked her letters.

Maybe he would really be her friend.

Chapter Two

Madelyn had never in her life had a drink before noon. She had never in her life had a beer at any time. It had seemed rude not to join him, however, and despite the fact she didn't much like the taste of it, the first glass did seem to relax her. And she definitely needed help relaxing.

They were seated on either side of the oak table and so far the conversation had revolved around Eddie's remarks regarding her apartment. When she told him that most of the furniture had come from her family, he said, "Yeah, okay—that's it."

"That's what?"

He was nodding his head. "I didn't think it was the kind of stuff a young woman would buy."

"Lots of young women are into antiques." She wondered if she could still be considered a young woman. She didn't think so.

"Are they? I didn't know that. I would figure they'd be into something more modern."

"Would you like another beer?"

"I thought you'd never ask." From the way he said it she got the idea he needed something to help him relax, too.

She put the two empty cans in the trash, then got two more beers out of the refrigerator. One more, that's all she was going to have. She couldn't believe she was drinking before lunch.

So far they had been polite, had been circling around each other. She decided to be honest with him and tell him what she was thinking. Well, not all of it, but at least some of it.

"I don't know about you," she said, sitting down at the table once more, "but this seems really strange to me. I thought I knew you, but now you show up and for some reason I don't feel any connection between your letters and you in person."

"Yeah, I know what you mean."

"Do you really?"

"For three years, you know? I mean, I thought I knew you better than I knew anyone. But now I feel kind of stupid, like maybe I shouldn't have just shown up like this."

She leaned toward him over the table. "No, Eddie, don't feel stupid. If I had been in your place I might have done the same thing." Might have, but probably wouldn't have. She couldn't remember the last time she had done anything strictly on impulse. Then she wondered if she was really that rigid, a bit of self-analysis that didn't please her.

"I thought of telling you. I guess I was scared."

"Scared? Of what?"

Eddie took a sip of beer, avoiding her eyes. "I guess I didn't want to give you the chance to say no."

"I wouldn't have..." she began, then stopped. "I guess I don't know what I would've said. You're going to think this is crazy, but for some reason I thought you would never get out."

He gave her a startled look. "What'd you think I was, some mass murderer or something?"

"I never thought about it. Well, maybe I did at first, but not after we'd been writing for a while. It's just that you never talked about getting out."

"You don't when you're inside. You try not to even think about it 'cause then you'd be making comparisons. You know, between the inside and the outside. And that's a sure way to frustrate the hell out of yourself. Anyway, I'm not a mass murderer. Not any kind of murderer."

"You don't have to talk about it, Eddie."

"You want to know something really dumb, Madelyn? If I had been a mass murderer I probably would've told you. Those kind of guys are nuts; they like to brag about it. What I did was so stupid I'd rather the subject wasn't brought up."

She waited, curious now about what he had done. But he was drinking his beer and looking as if the subject had now been covered. So she did what she should have done three years ago; she asked, "What *were* you in for?"

He grinned then and she was amazed at how it changed his face. "Got you wondering now, don't I?"

He had, but she didn't want him to think it was all that important to her, even though it was beginning to be. She shrugged. "I can't believe you did anything very bad."

"Bad enough to get seven years. You can kill a person and get off with less time."

Or a number of other things she would rather not think about. "Did you kill someone?" She tried to sound casual, as though it were something she asked everyone.

"No. But I'll tell you, there were a few times in prison when I sure felt like it. Particularly the first year."

"Everyone feels like it sometimes."

"No, not everyone. I'll bet you've never felt like killing anyone, Madelyn."

She tried to think of some occasion when she had, so she could tell him about it, but she couldn't think of one. "Did you hurt anyone?"

"Look, let's get it out of the way before you imagine worse than it was. I robbed a bank, okay?"

Though a law-abiding person, Madelyn nonetheless found the idea of robbing a bank rather romantic. A modern-day Billy the Kid sitting in her apartment. Drinking a few beers with Jesse James.

"Why are you smiling?"

Madelyn stopped smiling. "It sounds kind of exciting, robbing a bank."

"It sounded exciting to me, too, but I was just a dumb kid. Now you look disappointed. What'd you want to do, Madelyn, rob a few banks with me?"

"No, of course not. I read this book, though— maybe I told you about it. It's called *Any Three*

Women Could Rob the Bank of Italy. I liked it. It was
really different. Interesting.''

"Did they get away with it?"

She nodded.

"I didn't. Maybe if I had gotten away with it, and
maybe if I was down in South America having a good
time with the money, I'd think it was exciting. But
what really happened.... Oh, hell, I wouldn't be
honest with you if I didn't tell you I found it exciting
at the time. But no more, I swear. Now I look back at
it and I laugh; it was something I did when I was a kid.
That doesn't make it okay, but I was really stupid in
those days. Anyway, the last thing I'd do now is
something that could land me back in prison. I
couldn't stand it a second time."

A bank robber. That didn't seem so bad. It could've
been something really terrible, something she would
be embarrassed even to ask about. "Would you tell me
about it?"

"Why didn't you ask me in a letter? It would have
been a lot easier to write about."

"I can always get you some paper and a pen."

He was grinning again. "I'd feel like I was writing
out a confession. Look, I'll tell you what. Open me
another beer and I'll tell you all about it."

"Do you think you should?"

"You're the one who wants to hear it."

"No, I mean three beers."

"Three beers are nothing."

She didn't see how they could be nothing when just
two were making her far more outgoing than she gen-

erally was. "Would you like a sandwich with your beer? I usually have lunch around now."

"That'd be great."

"Pastrami?"

"Perfect."

She got up from the table. "Tell me about it while I fix the sandwiches."

"I guess I ought to tell you the whole story. I mean, robbing that bank wasn't the first thing I ever did. I've been in and out of jails and reform schools since I was about twelve, which is one of the reasons I got so much time for a bank robbery. It was a lot of little stuff—the worst was stealing a car—but if I had been out of reform schools as much as I was in them, I might've done worse. I would've had more time."

"You don't have to tell me all this."

"I know. I just want you to understand that I didn't just rob some bank out of the blue. It was all leading up to something like that. By that time I guess I had this attitude that stealing was easier than working, that only jerks got jobs. I figured I was too smart for that. Still, if it hadn't been for River Rat—"

"*What?*" Madelyn turned around to look at him.

"He was called River Rat. His real name was Michael Rivers, but he got the name River Rat and that's all we ever called him."

"What were you called?"

"Eddie. I never had a nickname. Well, yeah—once I had one, but it wasn't the kind of thing I'd want to repeat. And the guy who gave it to me—well, I made sure he went back to calling me Eddie real quick. Anyway, River Rat was a couple of years older than me and I thought he knew everything there was to know. So when he started talking about this bank job he was planning I told him I wanted in. And when he said yeah, that just the two of us could pull it off, I figured I had the world by the tail. I mean, Rat was talking about hundreds of thousands of dollars and how we could go to South America and live like millionaires for the rest of our lives. I pictured beaches, good weather, maybe a Mustang convertible.''

She put the sandwiches on plates and set them on the table and was disappointed when he stopped talking and started to eat. She was torn between being rude and questioning him and letting him eat in peace when the ringing of the phone decided it for her.

She knew it was her mother before answering. Her mother always called her during her lunch hour at work to see how she was. Madelyn usually looked forward to the calls, but now she found it an intrusion.

''Hello, Mother,'' she said as soon as she picked up the phone.

That wasn't her usual way of answering the telephone and it must have surprised her mother. ''Well, you sound happy today. What are you doing, darling?''

''Just eating lunch. Pastrami. Actually, a pastrami sandwich on rye with a beer.''

There was a long silence. ''Beer? I didn't know you liked beer.''

''I didn't at first but I'm beginning to.''

''I see. Are you alone, Madelyn?''

For the first time in her life, Madelyn lied outright to her mother. "Of course I'm alone." Then she wondered what her mother would say if she told her she was alone with an ex-convict who just happened to stop by.

"Your father's birthday is Saturday, dear. We're expecting you for dinner."

"I know, Mother. You've already reminded me about six times."

"You don't sound like yourself, Madelyn. Why don't you call me tonight, and we'll have a nice talk."

"All right, Mother."

When she went back to the table Eddie was smiling. "Alone, huh?"

"Mother would never understand."

"Does she know you've been writing to me?"

Madelyn shook her head. "This'll probably sound silly to you, but I wanted to keep it private."

"I did, too. Most of the guys used to talk about their letters, but I never talked about yours."

She didn't know why, but that made her happy. "I see you finished your sandwich. You want another?"

"No, thanks. But that was a real treat. You wouldn't believe the garbage they served us."

"Go on. Tell me about the bank robbery."

"You're really set on hearing about it, aren't you?"

"I find it fascinating."

"I don't want you to find it fascinating. Here I am, determined to go straight and act like a responsible adult, and you find bank robbers fascinating."

She found she was already feeling enough at ease with him to joke a little. "I didn't say I found robbers fascinating. Just the robbery. Maybe. For all I know yours was pretty boring.''

"It was. It was this savings-and-loan in the town where we lived. Rat's cousin had this apartment about two blocks from the bank and he let us borrow it for a couple of days. Well, we gave him a few bucks for the use of it. And that was it. We moved into the apartment and the next day we robbed the bank.''

"That's it?''

"That's it.''

"There had to be more to it than that.''

"Okay, you want it all? We got up in the morning; we walked to the bank; I stood at the door holding a fake gun on all the people while Rat got the money, and then we walked home.''

She couldn't help smiling. "You *walked*? You didn't have a getaway car?''

"You see too many movies.''

"Oh, come on, Eddie, you just walked home with the money?''

"It was only two blocks. Anyway, it worked.''

"If it worked, how come you went to prison?''

"It would've worked if the cops hadn't been looking for Rat's cousin, which he had somehow neglected to tell us. What was really funny was the window to the apartment overlooked the bridge going over the river, leading out of town. So we got back there and we were counting the money and while we were doing that we could see the police putting up roadblocks on the bridge to catch the bank robbers when they tried to get out of town. And we were sitting there watching them. Except these other cops,

who were looking for Rat's cousin over some proba-
tion violation, came to the door, and when we opened
the door they saw this money all over the place. We
had been covering each other with it and laughing like
crazy. You know, like you do with sand at the beach."

"How old were you?"

"Nineteen."

That made him about twenty-nine now and younger than her by a couple of years. It shouldn't have
bothered her, but it did. She thought she could picture him at nineteen. Just a kid playing at being a big-
time criminal.

"Ten years seems like a long time for a bank robbery with a fake gun."

"I would've been out sooner. I got three years
added on for hitting a guard. That was about my third
month in. He was asking for it, and I had this hot
temper in those days. You wouldn't have liked me
when I was a kid; I was always getting into fights. Not
that that was anything unusual where I grew up. Hell,
you probably don't like me now."

Madelyn had an urge to reach over and take his
hand, but she didn't. "I liked you very much in your
letters, Eddie. And you're not a kid now."

"Don't get me confused with one of the characters
in those books you read. I know a lot of books make
criminals sound real interesting, but if you met the
ones I've met, you wouldn't think so. For the most
part they're just people who can't get along in the real
world. Losers."

Madelyn, who had never functioned very well in the
real world, finished her beer and then sat in silence.

"See, I shouldn't have told you."

"Why?"

"Because now you're looking at me like I'm some strange animal in a zoo."

"That's not what I think at all." But he would never understand that she found having lunch with a bank robber highly romantic. It was exactly like something that might occur in a book, and not anything like what usually occurred in her life, which was just about nothing. And maybe five percent of the pleasure was in knowing that both her parents would have had heart attacks if they knew what their daughter was doing at the moment.

EDDIE WAS PRETTY SURE that she was just being polite about what she thought. But there was no use in pretending to her that he wasn't an ex-con, because she knew better. Not that he would offer that piece of information to anyone else if he could help it. As least he was glad now he was a bank robber. If he had killed someone he was sure she would be looking at him in ways a lot worse. In fact, she'd probably be scared stiff.

He saw her look at the clock and got the feeling he was about to be dismissed. That was okay. He had seen her, he thought they'd got along pretty well, and maybe he'd be able to see her again. He hoped he'd get to see her again. Three years of letter writing had to mean something. It did to him.

He was thinking about getting up when Madelyn said, "I have to go by my grandmother's and see how she is. Would you like to come along?"

That kind of threw him. "You don't mind your grandmother meeting me?"

"I don't imagine she'll ask about your bank robbery."

"Don't worry, I won't bring it up. Look, I know I've been away for a long time, but even I know these clothes must look pretty strange. It's what they gave me to leave in."

Madelyn's eyes were alight and he was pretty sure she was feeling the beer. "If you think you look strange, wait until you see Babba."

"Babba?"

"That's what we call her. Come on, it'll be a nice walk; I'll show you the neighborhood. You're going to find you're one of the least strange-looking people in the Village."

Eddie didn't like the idea of looking even a little strange. "You in a hurry?" he asked her. She was putting on her coat and he thought it was a good color for her. It brought out the red highlights in her hair and made her skin look the color of ivory dice.

"No. I just stop by sometime in the afternoon, that's all. Babba doesn't have a phone, so we can't call her to see how she is. She's in good shape for eighty-three but you never know at that age."

"I would've figured everyone in the city would have a phone."

She smiled. "Everyone but Babba. She got in a dispute with the phone company when she wanted an unlisted phone number and found out they charged for it. She thinks everyone should be unlisted and the charge should be for appearing in the book."

Eddie thought that made sense. "She won't mind my coming along with you?"

"She'll love it. If I thought she would mind, I wouldn't have asked. But I do have to stop by, and that way we can talk a while longer."

"I just figured, if you're not in a hurry, I wouldn't mind buying some clothes. Just some Levi's, maybe a sweater. I feel like I got ex-con written all over me in these clothes."

She was looking him over carefully, and he saw her eyes pause at the wide lapels on his suit jacket. "I don't pay much attention to clothes, so I could be wrong, but I think what you're wearing would be considered trendy in Babba's neighborhood. They have all these vintage clothing stores over there, and the jackets I've seen look just like that."

Trendy. He didn't want to look trendy, whatever that was, any more than he wanted to look like he just got out of the joint.

He put on his coat and followed her down to the street, where he immediately felt a sense of anxiety. He thought, again, that it was the speed of things. If something moved fast in prison, watch out. Now he couldn't seem to rid himself of the sense of danger every time he caught any fast movement in his peripheral vision.

The street they were walking down had one men's clothing store after another but the clothes didn't look right to him. For that matter, the men they passed were dressed in a way that didn't look right to him. And then he remembered they were in Greenwich Village. Everyone knew about Greenwich Village.

Yeah, now that he thought about it, the men they passed were checking him out, not Madelyn. He just hadn't noticed it before because it wasn't that uncommon in prison. You just ignored it, that's all, or maybe gave the guys a little lip.

When they reached a main thoroughfare, Eddie glanced at a street sign and saw it was Seventh Avenue. The sidewalk was pretty crowded, and when someone bumped into him, he immediately reacted by whirling around, then remembered where he was and gave Madelyn a sheepish grin. "It's all the sudden movements; I can't get used to it."

"It'll probably just take a little time," she said, and then he felt her hand slipping into his and he found that just holding hands with her felt reassuring. Like nothing bad would happen.

They didn't talk much. He was too busy looking at everything and Madelyn would occasionally point out something to him, but mostly she just kept quiet. That was okay. He didn't like constant talking himself. He had a lot he wanted to say to her, a lot he wanted to ask her, but there was no hurry. He just wanted to take it slow and easy in really getting to know her.

A few blocks farther on they cut through a park and he noticed that the guys were dressed differently there. More normal. For the most part jeans and jackets, and all of them seemed to be wearing running shoes.

"Those kinds of clothes," he said to her, and when she gave him a questioning look, he said, "I just want to look like these guys. Normal, you know?"

"They're mostly college kids," she told him. "Most of this area is NYU," and at his questioning look, she added, "New York University."

When they reached St. Mark's Place it was a different world. He had thought some of the people in the Village dressed strange, but now he figured he hadn't even seen strange until this. "What're they supposed to be?" he asked her, nodding in the direction of some young people.

"Punk rockers," she told him. "That's what you need, Eddie, some streaks of color in your hair."

He looked to see if she was serious and caught her smile. "Your grandmother lives around here?"

She nodded. "She's lived here for over sixty years. This used to be the Lower East Side, and it was dirt cheap to live here; now they call it the East Village, and this street, at least, has become trendy."

"You keep using that word. 'Trendy.' What exactly does it mean?"

"Oh, it means what's 'in,' up-to-date. New and popular, I guess."

He was looking around. "I wouldn't figure an old lady living here."

"That's because you haven't met Babba."

He decided he couldn't wait to meet Babba.

MADELYN WAS SMILING to herself when she let herself in with her key, then stood aside so Eddie could enter. Eddie had probably met some pretty strange people in prison, but she would bet he had never met anyone quite like Babba. Inviting him along to meet her grandmother had been a spur-of-the-moment thing;

she did it partly because she wanted to keep Eddie with her longer, and partly because she thought Eddie and Babba might get along. It would have been different if it had been her parents she was visiting. But Babba wasn't on good terms with her daughter and son-in-law, so it wasn't likely the news of Eddie would reach them.

Her grandmother's apartment had always been a part of Madelyn's life, but now she tried to see it through Eddie's eyes. It was a railroad flat, three rooms in a row that opened on one another, and each one was stuffed to capacity with books and pamphlets and stacks of newspapers that were taller than Babba. Even the walls were a mosaic of newspaper clippings that Babba had taped up over the years. The only furniture was a narrow bed in the bedroom, a table and two chairs in the kitchen, and a horsehair sofa of ancient vintage in the living room.

And then, of course, there was Max, seated on the other end of the sofa from Babba. Babba herself looked outrageous today, in psychedelic colors that fairly assaulted the senses.

Madelyn looked around at Eddie to try to assess his reaction, but he hadn't caught sight of Babba yet and was instead running his hand over a pile of books. "I hope the sight of all this doesn't send you running back to prison," she said, leading him in a circuitous route around the towering stacks of books and into the living room. She heard his chuckle and looked around again.

"I see where you got your love of books," he said.

Her grandmother was writing in a notebook and ignoring her arrival, which didn't bode well. The headphones to her Sony Walkman were in place over her ears. "Babba," Madelyn said loudly, "this is my friend Eddie Mello. Eddie, this is my grandmother, Frances Alling."

This got Babba's attention, as well it should. Madelyn visited her every day and never before had brought along a friend. Dark eyes under stark black bangs that needed trimming looked up and fixed on Eddie—a rather astonished-looking Eddie, who probably thought he had seen everything before.

"How do you do, Mrs. Alling?" said Eddie, keeping his distance. And Madelyn watched as Eddie's eyes were inexorably drawn to Max.

"*Ms*. Alling," corrected Babba, who seemed to be in somewhat of a sour mood.

Madelyn sat down on a stack of books and motioned Eddie to another. "Is the letter ready to be mailed?"

Babba ignored her.

Madelyn turned to Eddie. "Babba writes a letter to *The New York Times* every week."

"Do they publish them?" asked Eddie.

"Speak up, young man," said Babba, her eyes still on her notebook but her ears obviously attuned to her visitors.

Speaking softly, and with a smile at Max, Eddie said to Madelyn, "Is that your grandfather?"

Babba shot to attention. "I requested you to speak up because you mumble, young man, not because I have any difficulty with my hearing. Nor am I senile.

Max is sitting there as a deterrent to anyone who thinks I am alone here at night and thus can be robbed with impunity. In case you have eye trouble, Max is a six-foot-tall stuffed doll, albeit anatomically correct in every detail.''

She could see Eddie taking another look at Max, who was attired in a three-piece suit today, and trying not to laugh. It didn't matter anyway, because Madelyn started to laugh and couldn't seem to stop. She was used to Max but could see how bizarre he must appear to someone unused to Babba.

Babba removed the Walkman from her head, which was a good sign. It meant she was open for a little conversation. ''I can smell the booze from here,'' she said to Madelyn.

Madelyn sighed. ''I had beer with lunch, Babba.''

''Since when do you drink beer, Madelyn?''

''Since today.''

''You could've brought me one,'' Babba grumbled. Then shifting her gaze to Eddie and back, she said, ''What're his politics?''

''I don't know,'' said Madelyn. ''Why don't you ask him?'' She had a feeling that Eddie would be able to cope with Babba.

''Well?'' said Babba, her gaze locked on Eddie.

''I've never even registered to vote,'' admitted Eddie.

As he was about to say something else, Babba said, ''Good for you. Nor have I.''

''Babba's an anarchist,'' Madelyn told him.

Eddie was looking more intrigued by the moment. ''That means you don't believe in any government?''

Babba nodded and went back to her writing.

"What about you?" Eddie asked Madelyn. "Are you an anarchist, too?"

Madelyn shook her head. "No, I believe in government. I don't always agree with it, but I like some sense of structure."

"I guess where I come from there were quite a few anarchists," mused Eddie aloud.

This got Babba's attention. "And where might that be?"

Madelyn held her breath until Eddie said, "New Jersey," and Babba looked satisfied with his answer.

"How's Shirley?" asked Babba.

"Mother's fine."

"And that man she married?"

"Dad's fine, too. It's his birthday Saturday. How are you, Babba?"

Babba gave her a look of scorn before putting the Walkman headphones back on her head and returning to her writing.

"We can go as soon as she's finished the letter," Madelyn told Eddie. "I always mail them for her. She won't do it herself because she doesn't believe in a government-controlled postal system."

Eddie was nodding as if he understood. "She likes private enterprise, is that it?"

"No, she doesn't like that, either. I suppose in her ideal society the mail would be delivered by carrier pigeons."

"I'm not overly fond of pigeons, either," said Babba, not missing a trick. "You can't even sit in the park anymore without pigeons walking all over your feet. Filthy, dirty birds, with no redeeming qualities.''

"What else doesn't she like?'' asked Eddie, clearly taken with the old woman's opinions.

"Let's see,'' Madelyn said, trying to make it sound uncontrived. "Prisons. She doesn't like prisons.'' Then she smiled at Eddie's startled look.

"Under anarchy,'' said Babba, "there would be no laws. And without laws there could be no crimes. And if there were no crimes, there would be no criminals. But since we don't live in a perfect society, there are prisons. Degrading, anachronistic establishments that should have been abolished years ago.''

Eddie leaned toward Madelyn and whispered, "That's my kind of woman.''

It was all she could do not to burst out laughing again, but if she had, Babba's headset would have come off and she would demand to know what the laughter was about. And even though she didn't think Babba would object to Eddie's record, she wasn't feeling up to listening to a two-hour dissertation on prison reform. Or abolishment. Or whatever.

When the letter to *The New York Times* was completed and read aloud—this one dealt with subway conditions—and then put into an envelope to be mailed, Madelyn kissed Babba good-bye and promised to stop in the next day.

"And bring your friend,'' said Babba.

The first thing Eddie asked when they left the apartment was, "What was that thing on her head? I figured it was some kind of hearing aid until she took it off.''

"You've never seen one before?"

He shook his head.

"It plays cassettes. Music. Babba thinks life should be like the movies, that it should have background music to it."

Eddie was smiling in appreciation. "I like that. Yeah. Prison would have been a lot better with background music."

Madelyn had the feeling that it should have been Babba with whom Eddie corresponded. She was sure that he would have found Babba's letters a lot more interesting.

On the other hand, with Babba writing him, Eddie probably wouldn't have been here today. He'd be in prison leading a revolt.

Chapter Three

His clothes appeared to blend in with the surroundings on St. Mark's Place, but as soon as they were back in Greenwich Village he felt he stood out. Maybe the Villagers wouldn't spot him for what he was, but if there were any ex-cons around he was sure they'd make him out fast enough. His clothes even seemed to smell like prison. He wanted to get something just to hang out in. In a couple of days he'd worry about buying clothes that would look okay for job interviews.

They were walking down Eighth Street, and it was filled with clothing stores. He slowed down in front of a window that was filled with different kinds of running shoes. "Would you mind going in there for a minute?" he asked Madelyn. He'd really like her help anyway; he had never been much for shopping when he was a kid. In fact, most of the clothes he had owned in those days had been given to him.

She was looking in the store window. "Of course I don't mind. Did you want to get running shoes?"

He shrugged. "I don't know. What do you think?"

"They're probably the most comfortable kind for walking around the city. And if you want running shoes, the prices here are as good as anywhere. Then, if you want, we can go to the Jean Warehouse. They're pretty reasonable and the college kids all shop there."

Inside the store he picked out a fairly plain pair in navy blue, then saw that the price was forty dollars, which seemed awfully steep for shoes. Hell, real leather shoes couldn't cost half that. Still, he figured they were waterproof and would be good in rain or snow.

He tried them on and they felt great—in fact, better than any shoes he had ever owned. He told the clerk that he wanted to wear them and to just throw his old ones away.

"But they look perfectly good," said Madelyn.

"Maybe, but they're a size too small. I don't think I could've worn them more than another block."

He brought a roll of bills out of his pocket to pay for the shoes and Madelyn said, "You shouldn't flash all that money around."

He grinned at her. "You think someone's going to rob me? You kidding? That'll be the day."

"And if they do, you can always rob another bank, right?" she said, but then she grinned and he could see she had been kidding. The clerk had heard her, too, but he was grinning right along with them as though he thought it was a big joke.

"Did you mind my saying that?" she asked him when they got out of the store. "You're not sensitive about it, are you?"

"Why should I be sensitive? It's what I did, is all. Anyway, prison knocks any sensitivity out of you pretty fast."

They were heading down Sixth Avenue to get his clothes when he spotted some golden arches and had the kind of longing he hadn't had in years, hadn't allowed himself to have. "Is that a McDonald's up ahead?" he asked her.

"Sure. You hungry?"

"It doesn't even matter if I'm hungry. I've got to have a hamburger. And some fries. That's something you really miss in prison—junk food."

She squeezed his hand and quickened the pace. "At least you don't have expensive tastes."

"These shoes were sure expensive." But they made him feel as if he were walking on air. He practically bounced when he walked.

She looked over at him. "Those? They weren't particularly expensive. I think the thing is, Eddie, that prices have gone up considerably since you've been away. You know how much movies are now?"

He shrugged. "A couple of bucks, I guess."

"Five. Even a phone call's a quarter now. And candy bars—well, forget it."

"I guess you're right. I know about some things, like the price of gas. But that's because it was always on the news. Other stuff, though, I guess I don't have a clue. What about a pair of jeans? They going to cost me another forty bucks?"

"Not unless you want designer jeans."

"I just want some Levi's."

Eddie should've been prepared but he wasn't. He could remember eating at McDonald's for under two dollars, but he found out those days were over. Still, the food was worth every cent, and that would be it for him for the day; he wouldn't need to eat again.

The Jean Warehouse had all kinds of men's pants he couldn't believe. Ones with funny-shaped legs and pockets on the knees, some that were supposed to hit above the ankle, and a pair, worn by one of the salesmen, where the pant legs were rolled up to beneath the knees and lined in plaid. Then he noticed the women looking at the same clothes he was looking at.

"Hey," he said to Madelyn, "are you sure this stuff is for men?"

"It's unisex," she told him. "Just about everyone wears the same things these days."

He looked around the store and saw she was right. Except for herself. She was dressed differently from the other young women he saw. He didn't know enough about clothes or styles to define it, but she looked more old-fashioned, more the way he remembered girls dressing when he was young. Plus, she wasn't wearing any of the crazy makeup he was seeing on other women.

He figured he was still about the same size he had been at nineteen, and he got a pair of Levi's to try on, then asked Madelyn if she would find him a shirt or sweater to go with it. "Nothing too trendy, though," he warned her, trying out the new word.

He was in the dressing room trying on the jeans when she handed him a couple of wool sweaters with crew necks over the top of the door. They were alike except that one was navy and one was khaki. He decided on the navy and walked out to show her. He didn't think he could go too wrong with navy shoes and sweater and blue jeans.

She looked pretty startled when she saw him and he said, "What's the matter? You don't like the blue sweater?"

She shook her head. "No, it's fine. It's all fine. You just look so different. Younger. You could be one of the college kids."

He looked at himself in one of the mirrors but couldn't see what she meant. But then he hadn't really had a good look at himself in the clothes the prison had given him to wear. "I'm going to need a jacket, too," he said, thinking about the gabardine overcoat three sizes too large for him.

"You should spend some time looking around for a jacket," she told him.

"I hate wearing that coat."

"I have a couple of leather jackets that would fit you, Eddie. You can wear one of them until you find a jacket you like."

Just the way she said it, so casual, as if she took it for granted they'd be seeing each other, made him happy. And if he borrowed one of her jackets he'd certainly have to return it; they'd have to keep in touch. "Okay," he said, and saw that she looked relieved, as if maybe she had thought he'd take the offer wrong, thinking he was sensitive again.

He ended up carrying the coat out of the store, not even caring how cold he would be. Then he threw it in the first trash can they came to.

"Watch this," she told him a few yards past the trash can. She turned around and he followed her look. "I knew it," she said, as they watched a man taking the coat out of the trash and putting it on.

Eddie was glad he'd made some guy happy. It had made him happy just getting rid of it. The salesman had put his old suit and shirt in a bag for him, and now he tossed the bag in the next trash can, but he didn't even wait around to see who would find it. "Now I feel like a new person," he said to Madelyn. "When my hair grows out a little you won't be able to tell me from the civilians."

"I can't now. Lots of men have hair that short these days. Except most normal people don't go around without a coat in this weather."

They were headed back to her place. It was getting dark out already, and he knew it was time for him to find a place to stay for the night. Then in the morning, he would find an apartment or a room somewhere—then go about trying to find a job.

It was going to seem strange living alone. He had never in his entire life lived alone. But even though it would seem strange for a while, the idea of living alone made him feel good. The idea that he could fix a place up just the way he wanted it, that he could have the kinds of food in the house that he felt like eating, that he could watch anything he wanted on television. That he could make decisions for himself. That he only had to be around people he chose to be around. That he could decide what kind of work he wanted to do, and not have it forced on him. Then, thinking about all

that freedom started to make him dizzy and he broke
out in a cold sweat.

As soon as they were back inside Madelyn's apartment with the door shut and locked, the dizziness
subsided and he recognized it for what it was: anxiety. He had heard guys talking about being anxious on
the outside, but he didn't think it would happen to
him. It worried him that it had, because the guys it
happened to were generally those who kept returning
to prison. Still, it could be that everyone felt anxious,
but it was only guys back in prison that he heard talking about it. The others, the ones who didn't return,
no doubt got over it in time, or learned to live with it.

He stood by the door while Madelyn went around
the room turning on lamps; then she put a pot of water on the stove to boil. "I feel like some tea. How
about you?" she asked him.

"Sure," he said, not really wanting to go just yet.
The apartment was so warm and cozy and safe, and he
wanted to ask her if she knew about any places where
he could stay.

He got his athletic bag and took it over to the couch.
Sitting down, he opened the bag and then heard Madelyn say, "You do have other clothes, then?"

"No. Just what I was wearing."

She looked at the bag. "Oh, I thought—"

"This is full of your letters."

Her eyes widened. "You kept them?"

"Sure. Every one of them. I guess you threw mine
out, huh?"

She seemed to hesitate, then she turned around and
opened one of the cupboard doors. He saw a bunch of

file folders inside and then he finally got it. "Those are my letters?"

She seemed a little embarrassed. "I was wondering if I'd need another cupboard soon, but I guess I won't."

He reached inside his bag and pulled out the wooden bird he had carved for her. Holding it out to her, he said, "I made this for you. A souvenir from prison, since I couldn't sneak out a license plate."

She just stared at it, and he finally got up and took it over to her. "I really don't have a talent for carving, but with enough time I guess it's possible to do anything. This was about my sixtieth attempt."

She reached out and touched it, and her face turned so soft he thought it might dissolve. "It's lovely," she said. "All that time—three years. All that time and I never sent you anything."

He put the bird in her hand and she held it as though it were alive. She might think the bird was lovely, but it was nothing compared to the way she was looking. He wished he could capture that look and keep it for himself. "I didn't need anything. Your letters were more than enough. They were the only beautiful thing in my life."

He could see that she was blinking back tears, and he went back to the couch to give her some privacy. "Hey," he said, wanting to get her to smile, "you could've sent me a hamburger, though. How come you never sent me a hamburger?"

She smiled a little then. "Next time I'll send you a hamburger. Even some fries."

"Yeah, but there isn't going to be a next time."

When she brought over the cups of tea, which was something he really didn't care for, he drank it anyway. At least it warmed him up some more.

Then the silence got a little awkward and he said, "I guess it's about time I left. What I was wondering, Madelyn—do you know anywhere I could get a room around here? I figure I'll look for an apartment in the morning."

"A room? You mean like in a hotel?"

"Yeah, or maybe a rooming house."

"I don't think there are any rooming houses. There are lots of hotels around, though."

"What would something like that cost?"

"I guess it would depend on the hotel. Probably anywhere from sixty-five dollars on up."

"What, a week?"

"A night."

"That much? What about a YMCA? Is there a Y around here?"

"There's one on Twenty-third Street. But it will probably be almost that much."

He leaned back on the couch. "Look Madelyn, can I level with you?"

"Of course."

"The thing is, I thought I had everything figured out, but what I didn't figure on, and I should've, was how much more everything costs than it did ten years ago. I got seven hundred dollars when I was released; it would've been more, but I spent a lot of the money I made in there on correspondence courses. And I figured a few hundred would be all I'd need to get an apartment and some clothes."

"Oh, Eddie, that's not nearly enough. An apartment alone would take more than that. They all want two month's rent in advance, and that's if you can even find a place. Then the utility companies will want security deposits. Look at this place. It's really only one room, but it goes for more than seven hundred dollars a month. Of course, rents are pretty high in the Village, but they're not cheap anywhere in the city anymore."

He couldn't believe he'd been so far off. All his planning, and none of it was going to work. "I guess maybe I should've stayed in Jersey."

"Do you have family there?"

He shook his head. "No, no one."

She had been looking about as confused as he was feeling, but now he saw another look on her face. He thought it was determination. "No, Eddie, you shouldn't have stayed in New Jersey. What you're going to do is stay here until you get a job and find a place."

"No way, Madelyn, I couldn't do that. I had absolutely no intention of doing that."

"I know. But if our positions were reversed, if I were the one who had got out of prison today, wouldn't you offer me a place to stay?"

"Of course I would, but that's different."

"What's different about it?"

"Well, for one thing, I wouldn't be afraid of a woman even if she had been in prison."

"I'm not afraid of you."

"Ah, look, Madelyn—just look around this place. You don't have room for two people."

"There are apartments this size all over the city with a lot more than two people living in them." And then he saw her mouth drop open a little, and he could swear she was blushing. "I didn't mean... Oh, dear— I hope you're not getting the wrong opinion of me. The couch you're sitting on—it folds out into a bed."

He wanted to reassure her. "I didn't think that, Madelyn, honest. I knew you were just being a friend."

"Would you get upset if I asked you something?"

"No. Ask me anything."

"Would it bother you to stay here?"

"I like to pay my own way, if that's what you mean."

"I don't mean that. I mean, there weren't any women in prison, right? Would it bother you to have me here?"

It took him a moment to understand what she meant. "You're talking about sex?"

She nodded, avoiding his eyes.

He couldn't help smiling. "What do you think, because I haven't had a woman in ten years I'm going to right away attack the first one I see?"

"I don't know. I don't know what it's like to be locked up like that for so long."

"Look, that's something else you try not to think about in prison. At least *I* tried not to. I've done without for ten years; I can do without for another ten if I have to. It's just not any big priority for me at the moment. Right now I just want to get used to being free."

"I appreciate your being honest with me."

"Listen, I appreciate your being honest with me. And I'll make you a promise. The minute I feel an urge come on to jump on your body..." he began, then seeing her expression, he added, "Hey, I was only kidding. I'm not a teenager. I can handle myself." But the thing was, he'd just as soon change the subject.

"Eddie, why don't you think of my apartment as a kind of halfway house. You can stay here for a while until you get adjusted to being free. That way you can take your time looking around for a job and not have to take the first thing you find. And, actually, it isn't a great time to find a job this near Christmas. The first of the year would be better."

"You work, don't you, Madelyn? I don't remember you ever mentioning it, but I figured you must."

"I'm not working right now."

"No?"

She shook her head.

"Maybe I could help you out, then. Pay my share, you know?"

"It doesn't cost me anything to live here."

Oh, God—he should have asked before. He shouldn't just go around assuming things. "Listen, if you got a boyfriend maybe I shouldn't stay here. I don't figure he's going to be that understanding."

She started smiling. "No, no boyfriend. I would've told you if I had, Eddie. I just mean I live here rent-free because my parents own the building. They own a bunch of apartment houses around here."

He had thought she was poor when he first saw the place. Or at least not very well off. Still, it was her parents who owned it, not she. She might still be poor.

"You got to let me pay for something or I wouldn't feel right staying."

"Whatever you want."

"One thing. What are your folks going to say about this?"

"I don't plan on telling them. But that reminds me, I was supposed to call my mother." She got up, and the next thing she did was to take the phone off the hook. Then she put it back on. "I guess that's not such a good idea. If my mother gets a busy signal all night she'll probably call the police to come over and check on me. I'll give her a call later. You want some more tea?"

"No thanks."

"We should've picked up some more beer on the way home."

"Look, why don't you tell me where to go, and I'll get some beer. That way you can have a little privacy and call your mom."

"Thanks. I guess it would be easier to lie without you listening to me." Madelyn went over to a closet by the front door and opened it, then said, "Come take a look. I think a couple of these jackets would fit you." She reached in and pulled out one in black leather. "What about this? It'll probably be okay because the arms are pretty long on me."

He tried it on, liking the feel of the soft leather. Surprisingly, it was okay in the shoulders, and the sleeves were just slightly short. "Yeah, this is great," he said. He had never in his life worn a jacket of real leather. He had always thought the fake stuff was just as good, but it had never felt this soft and comfortable.

"Good. Okay, when you get out of the building, turn right and go to the corner. There's a deli there that carries beer. And if you need anything like a toothbrush or shaving stuff, they have that, too."

He opened the door and stood there for a moment. "This is real nice," he said.

"What's real nice?"

"Knowing I have a place to come back to."

She reached out and gave him a quick hug. A nice hug, the kind a friend would give. "See you in a little while, Eddie."

SHE LEANED BACK against the door and hugged herself with delight. She had been hoping he would stay in New York. And if he was going to stay in the city, she had been further hoping that maybe he would find a place nearby. Near enough so that they could see each other easily. What she hadn't even dreamed of was that he would stay with her.

She was still astounded that she had asked him to. In the three years she had lived there, she had never even had a man in her apartment. Well, her father, but he didn't count. And now, the first man even to visit her she had asked to move in with her. Yet that shouldn't seem so strange. She felt she knew him better than she had ever known anyone.

In a sense she felt responsible for him. He was so alone and appeared to be bewildered by everything at once. She had felt protective of him when they had been outside and she could feel him tense up every time someone brushed up against him on the sidewalk. And he had seemed so unsure of his own judgment in the stores. One on one he was okay, and he had been a delight at Babba's, but in crowds he appeared uneasy. And New York was always crowded.

It would be nice to have a friend staying with her. She could show him the city and teach him how to get around, and they could see movies together and shop for more clothes for him. She would have someone to eat with and to talk to and they would get a chance to know each other in person as well as they had come to know each other in letters.

Her parents shouldn't be a problem. If she was careful, they would never have to find out. They rarely visited her, and because their loft was so much bigger, she usually went there. And there would be no reason for Eddie ever to answer the phone. Christmas might be a problem, but by then she would ask if she could bring a friend along to dinner. Someone who was new to the city and had no family to go to for the holidays.

Christmas. She thought of hanging up two stockings in front of the fireplace, maybe walking to Washington Square to sing carols, then waking up on Christmas morning and opening presents. During the three years she had written to him she had sometimes wondered whether she should instead be out meeting people. Now she knew she had done the right thing, because it had all been leading up to this moment.

She called her mother and made it brief, saying there was a movie she wanted to watch on television. Her mother mentioned her father's birthday again before hanging up, but Madelyn didn't think that would be a problem, either. Eddie would probably enjoy an evening alone, a little privacy. It was something they weren't going to have much of in such close quarters.

She hoped he wouldn't question her too much about her personal life. It always embarrassed her to have to admit to people that she didn't work. On the occasions this had happened, mostly with friends she'd made in the classes she took, she could detect jealousy, a sense that they wished they could be supported by their parents and just do what they wanted. Sometimes, though, she just got an odd look, a look that said they couldn't define her if she didn't work, that a nonworking person was in ways a nonentity.

She made new friends with each class, never retaining the old ones. They seemed to disappear: back to their jobs, back to their social lives, and on the few occasions Madelyn had called someone later, the former classmate never suggested that they get together.

She knew she was different. Most of the women she had met either worked and had a social life, which revolved around meeting men, or worked and were married and no longer were looking for a social life outside of their homes. She found she only minded this difference when she was with these people. On her own, she enjoyed not having to compete in some job or hang out in bars to meet men. She liked her quiet life.

And now, there was Eddie coming into that quiet life. Inexplicably, she thought he would fit in perfectly.

When he returned he had two six-packs of beer and a bag of potato chips, plus numerous toiletries, and she cleared out a shelf in the medicine cabinet for him. Then she put some records on the stereo, and they both sat down to drink a beer and relax.

"What time do you go to bed?" he asked her at one point.

"Anytime I like." She looked over at him and saw a look of awe on his face.

Then he said, "Anytime you like. That sums it up right there, Madelyn. That's what freedom is—going to bed anytime you like." He laughed in delight.

"I also eat anytime I like."

"What about getting up in the morning?"

She laughed. "Anytime I like. Of course, it's not going to be the same with you here. We'll probably have to compromise."

"If you mean I might be used to going to bed early, don't worry about it. If I can sleep through a prison riot, your making some noise isn't going to bother me."

Her eyes grew large. "There were riots?"

"No, not really. Not where I was. It was damn noisy, though."

"I'm pretty quiet."

"I figured you were."

"How could you figure that? I wrote those long letters and you thought I was quiet? I would've thought you'd get the idea I talked all the time."

"People who talk all the time don't have time left over to write letters."

"What'd you think I looked like?"

"I didn't think much about it. It didn't matter. Why? Did you have me pictured?"

She smiled. "Yes, but I thought you'd look like Clint Eastwood."

He chuckled. "Sorry to disappoint you. Not that I'd mind looking like Clint Eastwood."

She thought he looked better than Clint Eastwood, more interesting, but decided if she told him so he probably wouldn't believe her. She had thought he would be older, though. He seemed older in his letters. It was going to bother her that she was older than he if she didn't get it out in the open now. If she waited, she might not have the nerve to tell him.

She just blurted it out. "I'm older than you."

"I don't believe it."

"I am. I was thirty-one a few weeks ago."

"Oh, I thought you meant really older. Two years is nothing. Anyway, you age fast in prison."

"You don't look older. You could pass for a college kid easily."

"I don't know about looks, but I feel older. It's like I went from being a teenager to an old man."

She was thinking about that, wondering if the longer he was out the younger he'd start to feel again, and was just about to say something about it when she saw that his eyes were closed and he was asleep. It must have been a long day for him; for all she knew he might have been up since dawn. He probably hadn't slept a wink last night knowing today was the big day.

She got up and turned off the stereo, then went to the closet and got out sheets and a blanket for him.

She touched him on the shoulder and he awoke instantly.

"If you want to brush your teeth or anything, I'll make up your bed."

"I fell asleep, huh?"

"It's okay."

"I don't want you to have to go to bed just because *I* can't stay awake."

"I don't mind. I'll just read in bed for a couple of hours."

She thought of offering him the loft bed, but knew that he would refuse it. Still, the couch ought to seem comfortable enough to him after a prison cot. And later on maybe they could take turns in the loft.

When he came out of the bathroom she had the lights off downstairs, but the light over her loft bed illuminated the room enough for him to see his way.

"Good night," she called down to him.

"If you want me to feel at home, you'll yell 'lights out.'"

"In that case, maybe I ought to lock you in the bathroom tonight. Then you'll really feel at home."

She heard his chuckle, then only silence. She looked over the edge of the platform and saw his eyes were closed. She climbed down the ladder softly and went into the bathroom to get undressed. He had bought a green toothbrush and it was hanging beside her pink one.

What was really going to seem strange, even stranger than having a man sleeping in her apartment, was not having a letter to write that night. She couldn't remember the last time she had gone to bed and hadn't written something to him, even if she didn't mail it until a few days later.

Still, this was better than writing a letter. This was real. Maybe she wouldn't even need her daydreams anymore.

Chapter Four

As soon as Madelyn left the apartment on Saturday night Eddie turned on the TV. She had left him alone in the apartment on several occasions: once to attend a class in current events at the New School; twice to see Babba, both of them agreeing that he shouldn't visit her grandmother with her every time she went; once when she went to the bank. Each time, as soon as the door shut behind her, he turned on the TV.

He didn't watch it; he just liked the sound of people's voices. He couldn't get used to the quiet. He didn't mind the quiet when Madelyn was with him. Lots of times they sat in companionable silence reading. But when she wasn't there, the silence had a different quality to it. It was the peculiarly dense kind of silence not at all like that of an absence of activity. It was the kind of silence that occasionally descended in prison just before some major trouble.

Already he thought he had learned her ways. For all that she had told him that first night about getting up when she liked and doing everything whenever she liked, she had a schedule that was every bit as fixed as the prison schedule had been. She got up at nine every morning; she had a soft-boiled egg and two slices of whole-wheat toast for breakfast, along with a glass of orange juice. She then did the breakfast dishes followed by a quick dusting and vacuuming of the apartment. Her afternoons were filled with visits: visits to the library, visits to Babba, visits to the butcher shop and the fruit market and the bakery. Two evenings a week she attended her class at the New School.

She was meticulously neat and organized. Everything in prison had been neat and organized, so at first Eddie didn't recognize this fact about her. But when he thought back to the foster homes he had grown up in and compared them with her apartment, he understood that not all women were that neat. She had reasons for it if he questioned her. Once when he had said, "Leave the dishes, I'll do them later," she told him you couldn't do that in New York, that if you left dirty dishes around, cockroaches were sure to appear. She was the same way with clothes and newspapers. A coat thrown over a chair had to be immediately hung up; a newspaper was thrown in the trash as soon as it was read. She said the place was too small. That in a big house one might get away with some clutter, but in a small studio every bit of clutter was magnified.

She was also very modest, but he could appreciate the necessity for this when they were living in such close proximity. The first time she saw him in his boxer shorts, though, he had to smile at the way she averted her eyes.

"Just pretend they're running shorts," he told her.

"It's all right," she said, but she didn't sound as though she meant it, and her face had turned a soft pink.

"Madelyn, I'm not going to waste my money on pajamas and a robe. Anyway, I've never owned either in my life."

"I said it was all right, Eddie."

She, however, never appeared in less than a full-length robe, so after that one time, he took pains not to let her catch him in his shorts.

When she left tonight she had asked him what he would do with himself while she was gone. Except for a couple of quick trips to the deli at the corner, he hadn't been outside alone, and he thought it was about time he tried it. So he said, "I was thinking I might drop in one of the neighborhood bars and have a drink."

He saw the look of disappointment in her eyes before she masked it with a smile. "That sounds like fun," she said.

He shrugged. "Maybe I'll just stay home and watch TV."

Her smile turned genuine. "I won't be late. I'll bring the Sunday *Times* with me—if they've delivered it yet—and some of Daddy's birthday cake. We'll have a party of our own."

At times like that Eddie got the feeling Madelyn wanted to keep him all to herself. That was fine with him. He felt the same way about her and was glad she didn't have a lot of friends coming over. He didn't think he was ready to meet a bunch of people, maybe have to answer a lot of personal questions. He liked it the way it was: just the two of them.

He went to the refrigerator, opened a beer, then, without having planned it or even thought about it, he opened the cupboard and took out a file of his letters. He carried them to the couch and sat down to look them over.

Sometimes, when he was in bed at night in his cell, he would think about the way their letters had progressed. He had kept all of hers, and by reading through them, he could pretty much tell what he must have written to get such an answer from her. Still, he had found himself wishing at times that he had copies of his letters to her so that he could read the questions and then the answers and not have to guess. Writing copies of the letters was too much trouble, though.

Now, as he read through some of his earlier letters, he discovered something he hadn't known. He had asked her personal questions at times; she, however, had never answered them. Even now, living with her, he realized there was very little of a personal nature he knew about Madelyn. He knew she had a grandmother, assumed she had two parents because that was where she said she was going tonight. He now knew what her apartment was like and some of her preferences in food. As far as her childhood, though, or her ambitions, or what kind of work she did, she never talked about those things and so far he hadn't asked her about them.

He hadn't been forthcoming about his life, either. Oh, he had told her about the bank robbery when she had asked, but he couldn't remember talking about

anything else personal. And yet, the surprising thing
was, they talked all the time. The way they talked,
though, was the way people talk who have known each
other for years and know everything there is to know
about each other. They spoke of everyday things the
way he supposed married couples spoke together. It
was a comfortable kind of talk, but not the kind where
either person learned anything new about the other.
He thought it was time they did begin to learn about
each other.

Eddie spent an hour or so reading his old letters
while the TV switched from a program with a constant laugh track to the movie of the week. He returned the file to the cupboard, didn't take out
another and, instead, found himself walking over to
the ladder to her loft bed and climbing up.

Hers was the first loft bed he had ever seen, and he
thought it ingenious. He sat down on the side of the
bed, then swung his legs up onto the blanket. He
bunched both pillows beneath his head and felt how
much warmer it was close to the ceiling, which might
account for the fact that she liked the window open at
night. He usually ended up cold, but since it was her
apartment he didn't complain.

He wouldn't have said that Madelyn had a scent—
at least, he had never identified one—but now, in her
bed, he could smell her presence. It was probably some
soap she used or maybe shampoo. Perfume he was
sure she didn't wear. Whatever it was, he could recognize it as belonging to her. He rolled his head over
so that his face was squashed against the pillow and
inhaled her scent. And then, with equal measures of

surprise and consternation, he felt himself becoming aroused.

He had thought he'd got his sex drive under control during the ten years in prison. Still, there was a big difference between living in a prison cell with only men around and living in an apartment with a woman. And there was no denying he was physically attracted to Madelyn.

He wouldn't have called her a sexy woman. She wasn't the type who got whistled at in the streets, but he had a feeling she could be if she wanted. She was tall, only an inch or two shorter than his five-foot-ten-inch height, but small-boned. He still hadn't been able to determine what her shape was like, since she wore layer upon layer of clothes and thick, woolen-looking stockings. Still, to wear all those clothes and not look bulky, she had to be slim beneath it all.

Her brown hair was thick and fell about her face, overpowering her small features in the same way her clothes overpowered her body. What he liked best about her features was her mouth. It was wide and thin and usually had an expression of childlike seriousness about it, and when she smiled it would turn down slightly at the corners, giving her smile some quality that made him want to hug her.

Eddie hadn't had much experience with women. He had never really had a girlfriend when he was a teenager. He had never been in a regular high school long enough to get to know a girl that well. The only kind of girls he had known were the type who were attracted to boys with a bad reputation, which he definitely had. They were never nice girls, the kind a guy might ask out on a date. They were the easy ones, the ones out for a few thrills, and since he had been out for a few thrills himself, they had seemed enough.

Madelyn was the exact opposite of those girls. She was intelligent and kind and decent, and he knew—he just knew—that if he were to try anything physical, make any move, he would do irretrievable damage to their friendship; like a small bird, she would become frightened and fly away.

He was going to be very sure not to do anything that would frighten her.

"WHERE ARE YOU, MADELYN? You certainly aren't here with us."

Madelyn looked at her mother and blinked. "What did you say?"

"You've been distracted all evening," said Shirley Shaffer, perched on the arm of her husband's chair.

Madelyn had been in the middle of one of her more recent daydreams. In this one she and Eddie were robbing the Village branch of Chase Manhattan. They were dressed all in black, with ski masks over their faces. Eddie was at the door of the bank with a machine gun and she was handing the note to the teller. Her mother had interrupted before she got to her favorite part, the part where they were flying off to Brazil with all the money and would live happily ever after.

"What's the matter with you this evening, Madelyn? You act as though you're thousands of miles away."

Madelyn looked at her mother, wondering what her parents would say if she told them she was dreaming about robbing a bank with the man she was living with. "I think I might be coming down with a cold," she finally said, hoping to explain her behavior and also provide an excuse to leave early.

"You getting enough heat in your building?" asked her father.

"More than enough. I keep the windows open most of the time."

"I'll certainly look into that," said Shirley. "What with the price of oil these days..." Her mother, who sold real estate, could get excited over things like the price of heating oil.

Madelyn made a move to get up. She knew that once she stood up it would take a good twenty minutes before she actually left. Her father would thank her once again for the shirt she had bought him; her mother would expect to hear for the third time how good the dinner was; Christmas would be mentioned and discussed; they would want to call a taxi for her, even though she could easily get one on the street. She was so used to all this she didn't know why it bothered her tonight. All she knew was that she missed Eddie and couldn't wait to get home.

Forty-five minutes later she buzzed the apartment to let Eddie know she was home, then ran up the stairs. He opened the door before she could even get her key in the lock.

"I didn't think you'd be back so soon," he said, locking the door after her.

"I told them I was getting a cold. Guess what I have for us? Croissants. Still hot. The birthday cake was something with lemon in it, not very good."

She handed him the paper, then hung up her coat and went to put water on for tea. "Why don't you pull the couch out? We can put our feet up that way while we read the paper."

When the tea was ready, she carried the mugs over and placed them on the end tables, then went back for the plate of croissants. Then, taking her boots off, she climbed up on the couch and piled some pillows behind her. "I love reading the Sunday paper," she said to Eddie.

She reached for the book review section, which was always the first thing she read. Eddie, she saw, was looking through the classifieds at the apartments for rent. She wasn't worried; he would see she was right, that he wouldn't be able to afford anything.

She was deep into a review of the latest Joyce Carol Oates book when he asked, "What kind of work do you do?"

She saw that he was now reading the help-wanted ads. "What do you mean?"

"When you work. What are you?"

"I've done different things," she said, wishing he would go back to reading. She had expected this question from him eventually, but she wanted tonight to be relaxed and peaceful.

"What kinds of things?" he persisted.

"Mostly selling."

"Yeah? You good at it?"

She thought of her last job at the dress shop. She had been fired the first day for telling a stout woman, when asked, that she didn't look good in a dress more suitable for a teenager. "No, I'm not very good at it."

"Why would you take jobs you're no good at, Madelyn?"

"I'm not good at anything. At least selling jobs don't usually require any experience."

"You went to college, didn't you? What'd you take?"

"I majored in business, but I hated it."

"Why didn't you change your major if you hated it?"

She shrugged. She didn't want to tell him that she had always done what her parents had wanted her to do, that majoring in business had been their idea. And they had been right about it being a good major for a girl at that time, when the business world was opening up to women.

"What do your folks do?"

For some reason she didn't want to tell him that her father owned a large printing company and her mother sold skyscrapers. It sounded too formidable, somehow. So she just said, "They're in business," and left it at that.

He put down the paper he was reading and gave her his full attention. "So tell me, Madelyn, what do you want to be when you grow up?"

"Oh, Eddie, can't we just read the paper?"

"I really want to know. Sometimes I think I don't know anything about you."

"I don't know what I want to be when I grow up. In fact, I'm already grown up and I still don't know." She wondered what he'd say if she told him she'd like to be a bank robber. That just about any other job she could think of paled in comparison.

"Didn't you ever want to be anything?"

"I've never had any burning ambition, if that's what you mean."

"Isn't there any kind of work that would make you happy?"

She looked at him, saw that he wasn't about to let her change the subject, and sighed. "I think I'd like to work with children." *If I can't be a bank robber,* she added to herself.

"You mean a schoolteacher?"

"No, younger than that. Little children. I really like little kids."

"Aren't there jobs like that?"

"Sure, in nursery schools. But they don't want people with business degrees."

"I would think, a business degree and all, some company would've recruited you in college. Isn't that how it's done?"

She nodded. "The thing was, I got sick in college, and after I graduated, it just hung on for a while." Not adding that by the time she felt strong again she seemed to have lost any ambition she might have had.

Eddie smiled. "It's crazy, isn't it? I'd love to have your business degree, and you don't even want it."

She thought he'd have more questions, but he went back to reading the classifieds and she returned to the review she'd been reading. She hadn't wanted to mention what her sickness was because they had called it the kissing disease in college, and she certainly hadn't got it from kissing.

She had also been afraid he would push her to go out and look for a job even though she wasn't pushing him to look for one. Maybe after the first of the year, when he started looking, she would go by some of the nursery schools again and ask about work. She was pretty sure, though, they wouldn't be interested. Anyway, she hadn't much liked the few schools she had visited.

She thought children should be in a cheerful, happy environment, but the nursery schools she had seen in the city had been dreary affairs with too many children and too few, too overworked teachers. Of course, maybe what the children really needed at that age was to be able to stay at home, but that just wasn't possible when so many mothers had to work.

She finished the book review section and reached for the magazine. "See any jobs?" she asked Eddie, who was still perusing the classifieds.

"There are a lot of jobs; it's just that I don't know how many employers are going to be willing to hire an ex-con."

"Do you have to tell them?"

He nodded. "At my age it'd look too strange not to have a work record. Anyway, I think they have a right to know. What would be perfect would be a place that would take me on in the accounting department and also pay for me to finish school, but I doubt I'll find that. I'll probably just take anything that will pay me enough to live and go back to school at the same time."

"You know what would be your best bet, Eddie? If you get a job at one of the schools, like NYU, you get free tuition."

"I didn't know that. Yeah, I'll look into that."

It wasn't much after that that she saw him begin to nod over the paper. He was still getting tired much earlier than she was, but then he'd only been there a few days. She began to gather up the paper, then got off the couch and carried the mugs and the plate out to the kitchen and washed them.

"Hey, I'm not asleep yet," Eddie protested, but he looked half asleep to her.

"That's okay, I want to get up early anyhow. I thought maybe we could take Babba out for brunch and maybe for a walk."

"Great, I'd like to see her again. Is she your mom's mother?"

Madelyn nodded.

"What's your mom like?"

Madelyn had to smile at that. "Nothing like Babba." He seemed to be in a questioning mood that night, and she expected him now to ask about her parents, but instead he went into the bathroom and she heard the shower being turned on.

She made up his bed for him; then, when he was ready to go to bed, she carried the newspaper up to her loft to finish reading.

Right away she noticed he had been up there. She always left the pillows in a certain way, and they were definitely out of place. She propped them up against the wall and leaned back, wondering what he had been doing in her loft bed. Not that she minded; she wanted him to feel at home in her place. Still, she found the idea of him in her bed somewhat unnerving.

More than that, really; she found the idea exciting. She moved her face against the pillow and thought she could detect his smell on it. Madelyn didn't have much firsthand experience when it came to sex, but she thought about it a lot. She knew she had an idealized version of how it was supposed to be, but it was a version that made her happy to contemplate.

And she'd be lying if she didn't admit to having contemplated it with Eddie. Apart from liking him very much as a person, she found the idea of his having been a bank robber highly romantic, just as she had found stories about Robin Hood or Billy the Kid romantic when she was a child.

Sometimes she wondered why he had never even tried to kiss her. She thought she would like to be kissed by him. Once, when they had been watching a movie together on TV and there had been a lot of kissing in it, she had looked over at him to see his reaction, but she couldn't tell anything from his face. Her reaction had been to wonder what it would be like with Eddie. Sometimes she thought that maybe being in prison for so long had done something to him so that now he was no longer interested in women in that way. Although, for all she knew, he might never have been interested.

He seemed content just to be friends with her, and that was all right. She had never had such a good friend; she didn't want that part of it changed. But she also didn't see anything wrong in affection between friends.

Maybe he was shy. Maybe she should be the one to kiss him sometime. Not a passionate kind of kiss, of course. More a good-night kiss. She always took his hand when they were outside, and he didn't seem to mind that. She would have to try a kiss, but not too soon. She would wait until he appeared completely comfortable with her. And if he didn't like it, she simply wouldn't do it again. But if he did like it, it would open up all kinds of interesting possibilities.

She pushed aside the papers and closed her eyes.

She and Eddie were walking into the Thirty-fourth Street branch of Goldome. It was a Friday lunch hour and crowded with customers. Madelyn took her place at the end of a long line, but Eddie caught her eye from his position at the door, reminding her with his look that bank robbers didn't have to stand in line.

Madelyn, perfectly cool and in control, walked to the front of the line, ignoring all the people's comments that she was "cutting in," and when the light for the next available teller flashed on, she marched up to the teller, handed over the note she had carefully typed up—along with the shopping bag from Macy's, which she handed over—then she watched with delight as the teller filled the shopping bag with hundred-dollar bills.

Shopping bag in hand, she and Eddie ran out the door and down into the subway station, merging with all the Christmas shoppers. That night they watched the news on TV and heard about the daring midday bank robbery.

Next stop, Brazil!

Chapter Five

The Communist Revolutionary Party was on one side, spouting their propaganda; a gay activist group was on the other, and several Moonies had their blackboards set up. Madelyn figured she could have started yelling that the end of the world was coming and half the people would ignore her and the other half would want to sign up.

Despite the overcast sky and chilly weather, Union Square was filled with its usual contingent of weird-os. Madelyn had been prepared for Babba's reaction; she had been here with her before. What she hadn't anticipated was Eddie's reaction.

"This is really great," Eddie kept saying, looking around in wonder, like a little kid at an amusement park for the first time. He was trying his best to see and hear everything all at once, and not succeeding. Then, with a look of devilment in his eyes, he began to egg Babba on. "Hey, let's hear it for the anarchists," he said to her. "Come on, make a speech, and I'll hand out some of those pamphlets you were showing me at breakfast."

Babba always traveled everywhere with a backpack on her back, and this backpack was invariably filled with the latest anarchist pamphlets she had single-handedly written, mimeographed and stapled together. Sometimes she even illustrated them.

Madelyn could tell at breakfast that Eddie took the proffered pamphlet from her grandmother just to be polite. He was hooked, though, by the time he finished the first page. Babba possessed something most fanatics didn't, and that was a sense of humor. Her writing, especially, was filled with wit and irony.

Eddie kept egging her on and finally Babba's eyes were glowing with fervor as she told him, "You should've heard me in *my* day, Eddie."

"Who says your day's over?"

Madelyn groaned, knowing what he was doing and wishing he wouldn't, but then she caught his wink and knew he was just having a good time, so she winked back, giving him her support. Then he was saying, "Let's hear a speech on abolishing prisons. That ought to draw a crowd."

"Especially in this neighborhood," Madelyn said, loving to see Eddie and Babba enjoying each other so much.

"I've been jailed in my time," Babba was telling him.

"What do you mean in your time?" Madelyn asked. "You've been jailed at least once a year for as long as I can remember."

"Don't tell me you're a criminal?" Eddie asked her, but Madelyn could tell from his tone that he didn't believe it for a minute.

"Depends on what you consider criminal," Babba replied, clearly enjoying all the attention.

"She protests things," Madelyn said, wanting to set him straight before he took it into his mind to start comparing jail stories with Babba.

"What things?" Eddie asked.

"*Any*thing," Madelyn said.

"Not anything," Babba argued. "Social injustices are what I protest. And wars. And governments sticking their noses where they don't belong."

"Which is everywhere," Madelyn added.

She saw that Babba was inching toward the group of communists, which didn't surprise her. Babba always loved to harass communists. Madelyn could remember being taken as a child into revolutionary bookstores and having to wait through interminable arguments. Communists seemed to like arguing almost as much as Babba.

Now Babba had taken hold of Eddie's hand and was leading him over to where one of the speakers was spouting the usual party line. Eddie threw a glance over his shoulder at Madelyn, and she smiled and nodded, then went in another direction herself until she found an empty bench to sit down on.

She was excited by the fact that snow had been predicted. There had been a couple of days so far when the rain had turned to sleet, but there hadn't been any real snow as yet. She thought it would be wonderful if it would snow so much she and Eddie would get stuck in her apartment for a week. She had always wanted to be snowbound, but in Manhattan the streets were always cleared pretty fast.

An old man on a bench opposite hers was feeding pigeons and they were all over the path. She agreed with Babba about pigeons. She personally preferred birds with the good sense to fly south in the winter. Pigeons were martyrs, preferring to stay and take their chances on freezing or starving to death.

She looked in the direction that Babba and Eddie had taken, and saw the crowd parting around the speaker to make way for Babba. Madelyn couldn't hear her grandmother's voice but was certain Babba was already speaking. She envied Eddie hearing her grandmother for the first time. She still enjoyed the way Babba spoke but had long ago tired of the subject matter, which was usually the same. Babba might make fun of the Communist Party line, but she had her own line of anarchism that seldom varied.

In her mind she saw Babba bundled up against the cold, maybe with an old-fashioned babushka tied around her head. She was bending over as she walked and looked old and frail, and when she spoke her voice had a discernible quaver. "Give me all your loot," Babba was saying, and the teller, astounded that an old woman was holding up the bank, quickly filled Babba's numerous shopping bags with money. Then, while Madelyn held a gun on the employees, Babba darted out the door and into the waiting getaway car, driven by Eddie. When they were safely away, Madelyn ran out into the street, snatched the wig off her head, and quickly mingled with the crowd. Later that night the three of them boarded the Brazilian airliner at JFK Airport and flew south.

"Madelyn!"

She opened her eyes to see Eddie grinning down at her, his hands stuffed into his pockets. "What's the matter?"

"Nothing's the matter; you've just got to see this, that's all."

"See what?"

"Your grandmother is single-handedly taking on the entire New York branch of the Communist Party."

Madelyn reached out her hand and Eddie pulled her to her feet. "I've seen it a million times," she told him.

"She's incredible. And you know something? She makes sense. I guess anarchism is the only way to really be free."

"It wouldn't work."

"I don't know about that."

"Eddie, it doesn't even work among anarchists. Get ten of them together and a leader will emerge. Have Babba take you to one of her meetings sometime." That's all she needed, Babba converting him to anarchism. She supposed she should have written him about Babba when he was in prison, sent him some of the pamphlets. It would have amused him if nothing else. On the other hand, the prison authorities might have found the pamphlets inflammatory and prohibited any further correspondence with her.

They walked over to the edge of the even larger crowd that had gathered as soon as Babba had taken over the microphone. "Has she done this all her life?" Eddie wanted to know.

"Babba's done a number of things."

"Like what?"

Madelyn found she didn't mind answering questions about Babba as much as she did about herself. For one thing, Babba was more interesting. "She's always been, well, 'arty' would be the word, I guess. She was a painter for a time in the twenties; then she got into poetry. When I was in high school she was involved in street theater. I used to live in fear that my friends would find out she was my grandmother. They used to put on plays right on the street corners in the Village. She also played the guitar and sang folk songs in a coffee shop during the sixties."

"Did she have a lot of talent?"

Madelyn thought about that for a moment. "Yes, I'd say so. I think she's very good at anything she does."

"What about you? You take after her?"

"I wouldn't even *try* to compete with her," Madelyn said, revealing more about herself than she had meant to. It was true, though; she shied away from competition, from comparisons. It was the same with her mother. Madelyn knew that no matter how well she might have done in business school, there was no way she would ever be able to equal her mother's phenomenal success. She didn't have her mother's brains or business sense anyway.

Madelyn heard the crowd's laughter and saw Babba being hoisted onto a large man's shoulders. There was scattered applause, and then Babba was let down and Madelyn and Eddie pushed through the crowd to her.

"It's snowing," said Babba, her voice sounding like a child's, and Madelyn looked up to see the first snowflakes of the season.

Madelyn held her mouth open and tried to catch a snowflake. "Oh, I love it," she said.

"It won't stick," said Babba, voicing her pessimism.

As the snow continued falling, they walked Babba home holding hands like children with Babba between them, the top of whose head didn't even reach their shoulders.

EDDIE THOUGHT IT FELT GOOD being out all day. Up until that day he had gone out with Madelyn occasionally, but those had been just short trips; most of the time they had spent indoors. He was getting more used to being outside now and didn't even flinch when someone bumped into him. Or maybe he did a little, but it was no longer out of fear.

Seeing Babba in action in Union Square Park had been a hoot. The old lady had more energy than he and Madelyn put together. Except for that, though, he hadn't much liked the park. He knew Babba saw it as a place for political dissenters to make speeches; he wasn't sure how Madelyn saw it, but she seemed mostly immersed in her own thoughts. As for himself, he could see crime all around him, and he didn't like it. He had counted at least ten drug deals in progress, and that had just been while they were entering the park.

It reminded him of prison and gave him an uneasy feeling, kind of like prison paranoia, which everyone got. He didn't ever want to be around crime or criminals again—he wanted to forget all that—but then he guessed he would have to get used to it in the city. And he had yet to hear of some utopia where there wasn't any crime.

When they dropped Babba off he figured she would ask them in, but Babba never seemed to do the expected. She appeared to forget them as soon as they reached her building, and without even a good-bye, she turned and went up the steps.

Madelyn reached for his hand and squeezed it. "It doesn't mean she doesn't like you, Eddie. In fact, she seems to like you quite a bit."

He reached out and brushed a snowflake from her nose and saw her eyes widen. "I've never had a grandmother. I don't imagine they're all like Babba, though."

Madelyn chuckled. "They're nothing like Babba. My dad's mother, she's about as dignified as you can get. My mother used to just die when Babba would show up at something like a family wedding. The funny part is, though, I think my other grandmother quite likes Babba."

Eddie thought he would have been glad of any grandmother, even an overly dignified one. But Babba, she would've been a real treat. Maybe if he had grown up under Babba's influence he would have ended up bombing a government building instead of robbing a bank.

"Is there a drugstore around that would be open?" he asked her.

"Sure, you need something?"

He grinned at her. "I think it's about time I taught you how to play gin rummy."

"You don't have to teach me. I used to play with Babba when I was a kid."

"Yeah? I thought only people in prison played it."

"I don't know," said Madelyn. "She could've learned it in jail, I suppose."

Eddie didn't know about Madelyn, and he didn't want to complain, but he was getting tired of watching TV or reading books every night. Both were okay, but they were the kind of things you could do alone just as well. He wanted to do something together with her. Also, TV and books were things he did in prison out of sheer boredom. Now that he was out, there were other options. Of course, he had played gin in prison, too, but he had never played it with her.

They stopped at a drugstore while he bought a deck of cards. Then, as they were passing a Chinese restaurant, Madelyn said, "Let's send out for Chinese food tonight."

"Why don't we just stop?"

"No, I'm not hungry yet. Oh, Eddie, don't you just love this snow?"

He wasn't all that big on it, but he nodded to make her happy. Then, passing under a streetlight, he saw her happy, upturned face, and stopped.

"What is it?" she asked.

He didn't know what it was exactly. All he knew was that he suddenly had this great urge to kiss her. He leaned over and, before he could have second thoughts, he kissed her cold, wet lips, holding the kiss just long enough to warm them. Then he started walking again as though nothing had happened.

She didn't say a word, didn't even look at him. He wasn't worried about it, though. Somehow, what would have seemed the wrong kind of behavior in her apartment seemed perfectly all right outdoors. Mostly, he supposed, because a kiss outdoors wasn't really going to lead anywhere.

He realized how good he was feeling. It had been a really great day, the snow was making Madelyn happy, and tonight they would have Chinese food, which he hadn't had in years—and then it had only been chop suey from a take-out joint in Newark. He thought maybe, all in all, it had been a perfect day.

Madelyn let them into her building; then she said, "Race you up the stairs," which was an unusual thing for her to say. He wondered if maybe the kiss had something to do with it.

They arrived at her landing out of breath and laughing, and it took him a few seconds after she opened the door for him to realize that there were two people in her apartment.

He looked at Madelyn, saw her stricken face, then looked at the good-looking couple on the couch. He was sure they were her parents. The woman had Madelyn's coloring, although she was much smaller; and the man had the same thick brown hair, although his highlights were gray rather than red.

"We were worried about you," the woman said, looking perfectly at home. "When you didn't answer your phone, with a cold coming on and all…" She let the words trail off while she looked from Madelyn to Eddie.

In a very tight voice Madelyn said, "Eddie, I'd like you to meet my parents. This is Eddie Mello."

Madelyn's father was standing and reaching out his arm, so Eddie took his hand and shook it, then told her mother it was a pleasure meeting her.

There was an awkward silence before Eddie said, "I guess I'd better go now. It was nice meeting you folks. Talk to you later, Madelyn." Then, without even stopping to think whether he was doing the right thing or simply chickening out, he let himself out the door and practically ran down the stairs.

He headed up the street and turned into the first bar he came to. He sat down at the bar and ordered a beer, then glanced unseeing at the TV set, which was showing the high points of some football game.

The bar was filled with more people than he would've thought would be out on a snowy Sunday night. When his beer came he drank it right down and ordered another. When the second one came, though, he let it sit there while he tried to decide whether or not he had done the right thing.

He thought so. He was sure it would better to pretend he was just taking Madelyn home than to act as if he were living there with her. And someone had had to do something, because Madelyn seemed half in shock. What he'd do would be to give her about an hour, then go pick up some Chinese food and take it home to her. They'd probably laugh about the whole thing together.

Then he began to wonder how long they had been there. And whether they had been in the bathroom, where his toothbrush and shaving equipment were right out there for anyone to see. That was probably all they had seen, though. The one change of clothes he had bought was in the closet, as was his bag. And Madelyn being so neat and all, the couch was always made up first thing in the morning.

He just hoped she was okay. Oh, hell—Madelyn was a grown woman; she could handle it all right. Except, sometimes she didn't act very much like a grown woman. And even though their living arrangement was perfectly innocent, he doubted whether her father would believe that.

She sure had good-looking parents. They looked rich and successful and a lot younger than he figured they actually were. He hadn't even seen any lines on her mother's face, although her father had some. But they had looked like the kind of lines you could get from being out on a yacht in the summer. Both of them had been wearing fur coats, which meant they couldn't have been there very long or they would've removed them. That was a plus. It meant they probably hadn't had time to go anywhere near the bathroom.

Maybe he ought to call her and find out if they'd left yet. A glance at the clock over the bar told him he'd been there only five minutes. It wasn't likely they'd have made the trip only to stay for five minutes. And if he called her and they were still there, it might fluster her.

Well, hell, he'd been meaning to go to a bar anyway. Or at least go somewhere alone. He knew he was getting used to having Madelyn go everywhere with him, and that wasn't so good. He was going to have to learn to function on the outside on his own. It would look pretty strange if Madelyn went job hunting along with him.

He looked around the bar. It looked like a friendly place, probably a neighborhood hangout, judging by the fact that people coming in seemed to know the others. It was a fairly young crowd, about as many women as men. He caught the eye of the woman sitting next to him, then looked away and took a swallow of his beer.

"You live around here?"

He looked back, saw that she was speaking to him. "Yeah, just down the street."

"I haven't seen you in here before."

"First time. I haven't lived here long."

She was cute, real tiny, with her hair cut as short as a boy's. She took out a cigarette and looked at him, then, by the time he realized she was waiting for him to offer her a light, she had reached down the bar and taken a pack of matches with the name of the bar on them. Not that he had any matches on him anyway, since he'd given up smoking about a year back.

"They serve good hamburgers here," she was telling him. "Broiled. Good steak fries, too."

"I'm eating Chinese tonight," he said, then wondered why he had said "I" and not "we." Then he wondered if the woman was trying to pick him up. He was flattered for about a full minute before he decided she was just being friendly.

"The snow's really coming down," she said, and he followed her look to the glass door. People were coming in, brushing snow off their clothes.

"You like snow?" he asked, wondering if she was like Madelyn.

"I do at first. Along about February I'll be wishing I lived in Florida. What restaurant are you eating at?"

"I'm not. We're ordering in." It felt good saying "we."

"You married?" She sounded disappointed.

"No."

"Got a girlfriend though, huh? Hell, I guess around here it could be a boyfriend just as easily."

"No, she's a girl. A woman." He hadn't thought about Madelyn being his girlfriend. Girlfriends were something you had in high school, someone you went out on dates with. If he were going to have a girlfriend, though, or go out on dates with someone, he would want it to be Madelyn.

He began to wonder what he was doing sitting in a bar when he could be home with Madelyn. He spotted a phone booth at the back and decided to call her. If her parents were still there she could always say it was a wrong number. Anyway, so what if they knew she was seeing a guy? That was perfectly normal. She must've seen other guys.

When he called, she answered on the first ring. She didn't even say hello; she just said, "Eddie?"

"I don't know why I ran out like that."

"I thought that was quick thinking. I was pretty surprised when I saw them sitting there."

"They still there?"

"No, they only stayed a minute. They were on their way to Lincoln Center."

"Why don't I pick up the Chinese food on the way home?"

"I've already ordered it. Where are you, in a bar? I can hear music."

"Yeah, just down the block. I'll be right home, okay?"

"Okay," she said, kind of breathing the word. Maybe it was because he had called it home. Maybe he shouldn't have said that.

He arrived at Madelyn's apartment just as the delivery boy from the restaurant was arriving, and he paid him at the door and carried the food upstairs. It seemed like a lot of money for a bag of food they would consume in one sitting, but it smelled so good right through the bag that he wasn't going to complain.

Madelyn took the bag from him at the door and he saw that she already had the table set. She didn't say anything as she put out the food, so he finally said, "What happened? Did they see any of my stuff around?"

She seemed puzzled. "What stuff?"

"My toothbrush and razor in the bathroom. I was afraid they might've seen them."

"What difference would it make? I use a razor, and I could easily have two toothbrushes."

He had worried for nothing. Still, they might have noticed his things and not said anything about it. They could be discussing it right now. And maybe he was too paranoid for his own good.

She dished out portions for them both, and he took a taste of everything right off and decided he liked it all. It was spicier than he'd remembered chop suey being. "That's a nice bar I was in; we ought to stop in there some night."

She ignored this and said, "The radio says there's going to be several inches of snow."

"You're really big on snow, aren't you?"

"I love it. I absolutely love it when we have a big snowstorm. I don't know how to explain it, but it makes me feel safe."

"Safe? Snow makes you feel safe?"

She nodded.

"Why?"

"I guess because everybody's inside, off the streets."

"No criminals out in the snow?"

"No anyone sometimes. You should see it when there's so much snow there aren't even any cars or buses around. It's so quiet and pretty. Everyone just stays home and builds a fire. The ones who have fireplaces. And I really love it when it snows for Christmas, although it usually doesn't."

One thing he couldn't help noticing: she was really into Christmas. She could get excited just talking about it. Him, he'd just as soon forget holidays like that. Christmas meant families, and he'd never really had one. In fact, his Christmases in prison had been the best ones he'd ever had. At least they had a good meal that day and usually something extra, like maybe a candy bar or two.

Maybe it would be different celebrating Christmas with Madelyn. Maybe with her it would seem real.

When they had finished eating and she had cleared the table, he got out the deck of cards and went over the rules with her. He wanted to make sure she knew them beforehand, like aces being low only, so they didn't get into an argument later on.

He found out right away that she wasn't much competition. Partly it was because she wasn't taking it seriously, but it was also the way she played. She never kept track of what cards he picked up, and she kept giving him cards he could use. When he mentioned this to her, she said she didn't care, that she'd rather give him something he needed than ruin her hand. That just wasn't the way to win at gin, but she wouldn't listen to him.

He decided gin wasn't such a good idea. For some reason, this was one thing that was better in prison. Probably because in the joint the guys really took it seriously.

Still, it was a break from the usual. Maybe tomorrow night he'd suggest to her that they go to a movie. Maybe stop in that bar afterward.

It would be like a real date.

Chapter Six

She was becoming obsessed with banks. First it was just the daydreams, innocent enough. Then one day Eddie bought a copy of the *Post*. Madelyn never read the *Post*. She was brought up to believe that *The New York Times* was the only suitable New York newspaper, other than the *Voice*, although even that retained some stigma for her parents.

They were stopped at a corner in front of a news-stand and the *Post*, faithful to its squalid mandate, had more of its usual deplorable headlines with a full-page picture of a baby being thrown out of a burning building. Of course, the baby had been miraculously caught by a waiting fireman, but one wouldn't have known that from just seeing the picture. It was the kind of story the *Times* wouldn't even deign to mention.

Eddie bought the *Post*, though, and brought it home, and she wasn't about to criticize his choice of reading matter. And, in fact, Madelyn took a look at it herself after he had finished reading it. And there it was on page six, just a paragraph under the heading

"Seven-Foot Bank Robber Strikes Again," but enough to catch her attention.

It seemed that some immensely tall man had been robbing branches of the Chemical Bank all over the city, but most particularly in Queens. After that she quickly scanned the paper for any more bank robbery stories, but that was it for the day.

When Eddie took his shower that night, Madelyn got the newspaper out of the trash and cut out the story, then slipped it into one of her files of his letters.

After that she encouraged him to buy the *Post*, although she never bought a copy herself. Just about every day there was another story of a bank robbery—sometimes two—and they quickly joined her first clipping in the file.

Bank robberies did not fill up her entire day, of course. After the game of gin rummy—which wasn't all that successful, since Eddie played it with such dead seriousness it wasn't even fun—they moved on to other games. Madelyn had Monopoly, which had been a favorite of her parents when she was growing up. She was never able to do very well against them, but found she played much better than Eddie, and they spent some enjoyable evenings playing.

Then, on the way to an Indian restaurant one day, they passed Lamston's and decided to go in to see what other games they might get.

Madelyn picked out Scrabble. Eddie wanted a game of checkers. Neither of them mentioned chess, which she was glad about. They considered backgammon and then decided against it. Madelyn knew it was vastly popular, but her own theory was that it was popular only with people who weren't intelligent enough to play difficult games.

They did get Trivial Pursuit. Eddie claimed to be a master at trivia, and Madelyn felt that, since she had read voraciously for so long, she wouldn't be bad at it, either. As it turned out, neither of them could answer ninety-five percent of the questions until the second time around, which made them think their memories were better than their knowledge.

Sometimes it seemed to Madelyn they were like a couple of kids who were allowed to play all day and stay up as late as they liked. At least that's how it seemed. And it was a happy time. They would get up in the morning, read the paper over breakfast and then argue about what game they were going to play. It got so they hardly even went out to eat anymore, preferring to order in, which made sense in a way, because the weather had turned unmercifully cold, with a wind-chill factor below zero, and it was no pleasure going out.

Their favorite game turned out to be Scrabble, and they would play it for hours on end. At first they played at the table, but because some games lasted so long they would have nowhere to eat, they finally took to playing cross-legged on the rug.

About four days into their game-playing binge the doorbell rang at about two in the afternoon. Madelyn froze. "It's my mother, I know," she said to Eddie.

He looked around. "You want me to hide? I could get into the closet, or go up in your loft."

Madelyn knew she couldn't ask him to do something that degrading. Instead, she got up, put on her coat and was out the door before her mother was halfway up the stairs.

"Hi, Mom, what're you doing here?" Madelyn asked her, taking her arm and practically forcing her to turn around.

"I hardly get a chance to talk to you anymore. You always have to get off the phone. I thought you could make me a cup of coffee and we could sit down and have a nice chat."

"Oh, Mom, I can't. I'm meeting a friend for tea and I'm late already."

"The young man we met the other night?"

"Who?" Madelyn said, trying to sound as though she couldn't remember. "Oh, you mean Eddie. No, I'm meeting one of the girls I went to school with. She's married and has a couple of kids now, so she doesn't get into the city too often. Going to the Plaza is a real treat for her." She knew she was explaining too much and it was probably coming out sounding like a complete fabrication, but she couldn't seem to stop herself.

Her mother managed to look both disappointed and understanding. Madelyn was just congratulating herself on her quick thinking when her mother said, "Well, at least we can share a cab uptown."

So there she was, riding in a taxi up to the Plaza. Her mother dropped her off, asking Madelyn to call her that night, and Madelyn was left standing out in the cold with no hope of getting a taxi for ages. And then she belatedly realized that she hadn't brought her wallet and didn't even have the money to take a bus or to call Eddie.

Walking fifty blocks in that weather should have given her the cold she had told her parents she was coming down with, but all it gave her was a couple of blisters and sore legs.

"What happened to you?" asked Eddie when she staggered in, teeth chattering.

Madelyn told him, and she could see he was trying not to laugh. Not that she didn't see the humor in the situation, but only later.

"Is this likely to happen frequently?"

"You mean my mother coming by?"

He nodded.

"I don't know. I guess it's possible. Maybe I should get the lock changed."

"She's your *mother*, Madelyn."

She thought Eddie had the idea that mothers were sacred, no doubt derived from the fact he never had to live with one. "I guess I'll just have to start talking to her on the phone longer. We used to talk every night."

"Well, I'll be getting a job pretty soon, anyway."

Madelyn didn't want to hear about that. She knew it wasn't really possible for Eddie never to work, for him just to stay home with her and play games forever, but she didn't want to think about that eventuality just yet. She guessed she wanted to make sure that when that time came, he would love being with her so much he would be eager to come home to her every night.

She took off her coat and sat back down on the floor. "Whose move was it?" she asked, getting a laugh out of Eddie.

EDDIE DIDN'T SAY ANYTHING to Madelyn about it, not wanting to sound as if he were criticizing her, and definitely not wanting an argument, but he could tell how phony she sounded whenever she talked to her mother, and he was sure if the woman had any intelligence at all, she would know it, too. What was more, her mother knew Madelyn far better than he did, so surely she would pick up on it.

So he wasn't in the least surprised when the buzzer sounded at eight-thirty one morning when both of them were still in bed.

"Oh, my God," he could hear Madelyn say, then he saw her peering down from the loft bed.

Eddie leapt out of bed. "It'll be okay. Say you slept down here last night and I'll get in the closet."

"No," she said, so loudly and firmly that he stopped where he was, his hand on the doorknob to the closet.

"I don't mind, Madelyn, really. I understand."

"I mind *for* you," said Madelyn, already in her robe and climbing down the ladder. "But I *would* get back under the covers if I were you. I don't think Mother will faint at the sight of a man, but she might at the sight of a strange man in his underwear."

Feeling strong misgivings, yet admiring her stand, Eddie got back in bed, but sat up, the covers pulled to midchest.

To say that Mrs. Shaffer took in the situation in a glance wouldn't be quite accurate. There were several glances at Eddie, several at Madelyn and one or two at the loft bed. "I knew something was wrong," she finally said.

Madelyn stood straight, a good six inches taller than her mother. "Nothing's wrong, Mother. Nothing at all is wrong."

"I happen to feel that lying to your parents is wrong. Did you think we would chastise you if we knew you had a boyfriend who occasionally spent the night? You're a grown woman, Madelyn. Your private life is your own business."

Madelyn, who previously had looked prepared to take a strong stand, now appeared to be crumbling. "He doesn't 'occasionally spend the night,' Mother."

"All right, I'm willing to believe it's the first time. It's still your business and not mine."

"He lives here."

Eddie was beginning to feel as if he were in a B movie. All it needed now was for her father to come in waving a shotgun and raving about his daughter's virtue. The funny thing was, he felt guilty as hell even though he was innocent.

"I see," said Mrs. Shaffer. "And how long has this been going on?"

"A couple of weeks," mumbled Madelyn, but clearly enough for her mother to understand.

"Is there some reason you didn't want us to know about this young man of yours?"

"I didn't think you'd understand," said Madelyn.

Eddie felt he should say something to relieve the situation. "The thing is, Mrs. Shaffer, I'm living here, but we're not exactly living together. Your daughter has been kind enough to offer me a place to stay while I look for my own apartment."

"You don't have to explain, Eddie," said Madelyn.

Mrs. Shaffer must have thought otherwise, because she approached the bed and looked down at him. Then she looked up at the rumpled loft bed, the blankets hanging over the side from Madelyn's hasty departure.

"Thank you for explaining, Eddie," she said. "Although I don't know why Madelyn couldn't have just said so. Have you been in New York long?"

"No, ma'am."

Mrs. Shaffer's mouth twisted in distaste. "Just call me Shirley, Eddie. Well, if you're not going home for Christmas, I want you to know you'll be most welcome to celebrate it with us."

"Thank you, I'd like that."

Professional smile in place, Mrs. Shaffer looked from Eddie to Madelyn. "Well, I'll leave you two, then. I was just on my way to work." She went over and put one hand on Madelyn's shoulder. "And darling, don't be so embarrassed. Your friend appears to be quite a gentleman; I like that."

Madelyn turned a mortified look to him as her mother left the apartment. "I'm really sorry you had to be put through that."

"I thought she was great about it. She could've ordered me out, you know. And I would've gone."

"Ordered you out of my apartment? I'm not a child, Eddie. My parents don't order me around." Although maybe they always had before. Before Eddie.

"Then why all the secrecy?"

"Because I was afraid if you met they'd ask you what you did for a living or how we met."

"Well, she didn't."

"They will on Christmas."

"Listen, Madelyn, nothing's going to shock them much after this."

"You're right," she said, starting to smile.

"Anyway, if you want, I'll lie."

"No, no more lies. I'm not ashamed for them to know how we met or what you did. If they can't handle it, that's their problem."

Eddie grinned. "You talk pretty brave when your mom's not around."

She walked over to the bed and looked down at him, in much the same pose her mother had used, her arms crossed over her chest and her head tilted to one side. "Oh, is that right? Who's the one who wanted to hide in the closet?"

"You're right. That was pretty brave of you just to let her in like that."

Then the unexpected happened. Madelyn sat down on the edge of the bed and grinned at him, looking very proud of herself. And although they had sat on the bed together countless times, they had never done it before when she was just in her robe and he was almost naked beneath the covers. She looked very soft and well scrubbed and pretty with her hair all mussed and falling down in her face, and he reached out a hand to brush the hair back but instead pulled her head down to his.

He saw her eyes widen right before he kissed her, and then they closed as she leaned against him, and it seemed like the most natural thing in the world for them both to be on his bed and kissing at nine o'clock in the morning.

He pushed her away for a moment as he pulled back the covers for her to get into bed next to him, and he said, "I guess we shouldn't be doing this," and she said, "I guess not," but she still crawled under the covers and they started kissing again, just giving themselves up to it, and he realized there was all the difference in the world between having sex with a girl you cared nothing about and just being close to someone he loved as much as he loved Madelyn. And that's what it was, whether he had admitted it to himself before or not. She was the only person in the world he could say he loved and truly mean it.

He wrapped her up in his arms and held her close and just kissed her until finally the need to speak overpowered his need to kiss her, and he drew her head down against his chest and said, "This doesn't seem possible. I didn't think it would happen."

"Especially not two minutes after you convinced my mother the whole arrangement was perfectly innocent."

He chuckled. "Yeah, I was thinking of that. Do you think I ought to call her up and confess?"

"To what? Kissing me?"

"I want to do a lot more than just kiss you, Madelyn." He wanted to, but after ten years he had to admit he was worried about his performance. Or, more specifically, whether he actually could perform. He had heard from some of the cons that abstinence did something to you, made you impotent or something like that.

And now Madelyn was saying that she wanted to do a lot more than just kiss, too, which meant that the theory was going to be put to the test.

"You mean that?"

She nodded.

"Not now, though." He waited, and when she didn't say anything, he said, "I think I'd like to wait until tonight. I'd like to have the whole day to look forward to it, to anticipate how it's going to be. Wouldn't that be a kick? Knowing we're going to do it tonight and going through the whole day just waiting for it?" Which was a chicken way of saying he was scared he wouldn't measure up to her expectations. As if prolonging it was going to help any.

She pushed herself up so that her hair was trailing across his chest, tickling him, even turning him on. "I think that's the stupidest idea I've ever heard."

"You don't want to make love with me?" he teased, purposely misunderstanding.

"I don't want to have to wait until tonight. Why don't I just pull down the shades and we'll pretend it's night?"

He couldn't help himself; he loved her too much to disappoint her. If it was what she wanted, he'd give it his best. He put his hand behind her neck and pulled her back down. "We've waited this long, what's another few hours?" He knew she'd argue him out of it.

"I didn't like waiting even this long, if you want to know the truth, Eddie."

And then, after all his worry, his wondering what ten years without sex might have done to him, he felt the slow arousal begin to build up and he knew for sure that he didn't want to wait any longer, either.

He reached down and untied her robe, then started to push it off her shoulders. She lifted herself up and helped him, finally pushing the robe off onto the floor. She was wearing some kind of flannel shirt, like a man's shirt, only longer, and it had buttons up the front. She was passive as he undid the buttons, then pulled it apart.

She was as slim and as lovely as he had known she would be. She had small breasts and almost no hips and long, pale legs, and her skin all over was as smooth to the touch as the leather jacket she had let him wear. He couldn't remember ever really appreciating a woman naked before. And then he realized that except in the centerfolds of magazines when he was a kid, he never had seen a woman naked. The girls he'd had sex with had never been naked. Maybe their bras were undone and their panties pulled down, but that was about it. It had never been lovemaking; it had only been sex.

He caressed her gently, taking his time, knowing he had all the time in the world. At his touch her eyes widened and she smiled, as though surprised at how nice it felt. Then he began kissing her again as his hands made their exploration, and she clung to him, returning his kisses with increasing abandon.

He found that of all the different emotions he was feeling, the one that was the strongest was that he felt as if he had come home. Sex had been nothing more than a cheap thrill when he had been young, but later, in prison, particularly after reading some book, he had got the sense that it should be more, that it should be maybe the greatest single experience you could have. And at this moment he knew with a certainty that he had been correct in thinking this; he knew that despite all the things in his life he had done wrong, this was going to be about as right as you could get.

MADELYN WAS FILLED with an excitement she couldn't contain. She found that she wanted to talk with him about the experience, analyze it. She wanted to share every detail, every feeling; wanted especially to compare feelings, to see if they felt the same way.

On the other hand, she wasn't sure if that was what she should do. Maybe she should not say anything— try to act cool about the whole thing. She tried to recall how people acted in books after making love for the first time. And because she was trying too hard to remember some instance, none came to mind. Then she realized that while she had been thinking so hard, he had already begun to speak and she hadn't heard a word.

"I'm sorry, what did you say, Eddie?"

He opened his eyes wide and let his mouth fall open in mock surprise, as though to chide her for not listening at a moment like this. "I'm telling you I love you and you're not even listening?"

She hugged the knowledge to herself for a moment, feeling a new kind of warmth spread through her—a different kind of warmth than she had felt during the lovemaking, but just as good.

"How can you love me already?" she asked, believing it but wanting confirmation, wanting a minute explanation.

"I think I was half in love with you before we even met."

"And just now you fell all the way in love?" Even though she had felt a powerful emotion for him when they were making love, she didn't want that to be the reason he had fallen in love with her. She wanted it to be for more than that.

"I don't know, Madelyn. I don't think I can give you an exact moment. I think it's been growing every day. I don't think I would have made love with you if I hadn't already loved you. I wouldn't have risked a friendship just for sex. Not that it was just sex with you, but you know what I mean."

"I thought it would be different," she said, expressing her thoughts without thinking about it first.

"What do you mean, different? Didn't you like it?"

"I loved it! I just thought it would be different."

"Different how?"

She put her face on his chest so that she wouldn't have to look at him while she spoke, and she liked the way his hair tickled her nose. In fact, she liked everything about his chest, about his whole body. She knew she was prejudiced, but she thought he was perfect. "I thought it would be more separate."

"I don't get you."

"I don't know, I just thought it would be me doing something and you doing something and it wouldn't connect that much. But it wasn't like that at all. I felt that I was you *and* me. Does that sound crazy?"

"A little."

She looked up at him and saw he was grinning. "I just mean that at times I couldn't tell the difference between you and me. Could you?"

"I guess I wasn't thinking about it all that much. I was just feeling it."

Madelyn felt chastised, as though she shouldn't have been thinking, either. But she couldn't help thinking. She wasn't going to go through an important experience like that without even thinking about it. If she didn't think about it, how would she remember it?"

"I don't think you had an orgasm," said Eddie.

"I did so!"

He chuckled. "No, I don't think so. Don't worry, you'll probably have one next time. And when that happens, I don't think you'll be doing all that much thinking."

Madelyn had a feeling he was right. She had been thinking so hard, savoring each emotion that buffeted her body, that she hadn't relaxed enough to lose control. Next time she would make very sure not to think.

Eddie ruffled her hair. "Don't worry about it. It's supposed to be fun, not something you get tested on afterward."

"I'm hungry. Want to order some breakfast from the coffee shop?"

Still holding on to her, Eddie pushed himself up so that he was sitting. "No, I think we ought to go down to the coffee shop, get some air."

She didn't think that was such a good idea at all. What she would really have loved was breakfast in bed, only they were out of food. Maybe what they should do would be to go to the grocery store and buy enough food to last for days. Then they'd never have to go out. Or even get dressed.

Eddie was giving her a knowing look. "Madelyn, it's not a game. We're not going to do it over and over so that you get tired of it, like you're getting tired of Scrabble."

"I wouldn't get tired of it." How could she possibly get tired of it?

Eddie sighed and took on a martyr's expression. "You're determined to wear me out, aren't you?"

"I would think you'd want to make up for the past ten years."

He gave a look of mock horror and said, "In one day?"

That made her laugh.

He got off the bed and reached for her hand. "Come on, let's take a shower."

"Together?" Madelyn felt excited at the idea.

"Of course together. No point in being modest now, is there?"

Madelyn couldn't see any point in that at all.

Chapter Seven

In Babba's words, "Christmas is free enterprise carried to its obscene extreme."

For years Madelyn had been trying to get Babba to celebrate Christmas with the family. Babba would have none of it. She didn't like the religious overtones to the holiday any more than she liked its rampant commercialism. Along with being an anarchist, Babba was also an atheist. In fact, the only way she partook of the holiday spirit at all was by eating the chocolate-covered marshmallow Santa Clauses that Madelyn would bring her. Babba devoured those with relish.

There was also the fact that Babba and her daughter, Shirley, disagreed about everything. Shirley's celebration of Christmas, particularly since it was something that hadn't been celebrated when she was a child, was just another indication of Shirley's having become middle-class. When Babba called anything middle class, it was meant as an insult.

So when Eddie, on one of their visits to Babba, suggested, more as a joke than anything else, that Babba could dress her anatomically correct male doll

as Santa Claus, all he got was a glare for his sugges-
tion. Madelyn had forgotten to warn him of Babba's
aversion to Christmas.

Christmas was exactly what Madelyn was there to
discuss that day, however. If there had been a subtle
way to bring it up she would have, although Babba
seldom understood subtlety. Madelyn decided just to
jump in and hope she could get through to her grandmother.

"Babba," said Madelyn, "I know I beg you every
year to have Christmas with the family, and every year
you turn me down, but I'm going to do more than beg
you this year. I'm going to plead with you until I get a
yes." The background information was more for Eddie's edification than Babba's.

Babba responded by turning up the sound on her
Sony Walkman. Eddie, delighted as usual by her
perversity, grinned at Madelyn. She didn't return the
grin.

"I think we ought to get her a Christmas tree," said
Eddie. "Just drag one up here, decorate it, and what's
she going to do, throw it out the window?"

"That's *exactly* what she'd do. Come here, I want
to show you something."

Still smiling, Eddie got up and followed her to the
entry hall, where Madelyn flung open the door to the
coat closet. The top shelf was piled to the ceiling with
brightly wrapped Christmas presents.

"I thought she didn't celebrate Christmas," said
Eddie, looking mystified. He must have thought
Babba had done her Christmas shopping early that
year.

"She doesn't. I, however, do. Every year I bring her a present, and every year she snatches it out of my hand, puts it in the closet unopened, and that's the end of it."

"Then why do you bother?"

"Because I love her. How could I *not* get her a Christmas present?"

He took her hand and pulled her into the closet. "I love that about you," he told her.

"Because I get her a present?"

"Because you get her one even though you know in advance she won't even open it."

She opened her mouth to say something else, but he moved to kiss her at that moment and she forgot what she was going to say in her sudden excitement. It never failed. All Eddie had to do was touch her, and some part of her she hadn't even known existed came to the fore, became the strongest part of her. It was Eddie who finally pulled away or she might have stayed in the closet with him and forgotten all about Babba.

They went back to the living room, Eddie saying, "I think she's right, you know. Lots of people say they think Christmas is too commercial, but they don't do anything about it. Your grandmother has principles and, what's more, she lives up to them."

Madelyn tore her mind away from Eddie's kisses and back to the business at hand. "I guess so. When it comes to that, so do my parents. They love the pure commercialism and they go overboard with presents. You'll see." Shirley stored up gifts from Bloomingdale's the way squirrels stored up nuts for the winter.

She started during the August sales and didn't let up until after the post-Christmas sales.

"And what about you?" Eddie asked her.

"I'm in between, I guess. I think it should mean more than just going out and spending money on everything you see, so I always make my gifts. It makes me feel good. But I never know if anyone really likes what I make."

"I haven't seen you making any Christmas gifts. Don't tell me you do it all on Christmas Eve."

Madelyn gave him a look of chagrin. "I haven't had time this year. I guess I'm going to have to be commercial and go out and buy them." She really hated doing that, though. Buying her parents' gifts with their own money didn't seem right, but since it was too late to try to get a Christmas job, she was stuck with it. Eddie, however, was a different matter. She was planning on cashing in one of her bonds for Eddie's gift; she certainly couldn't expect her parents to pay for that.

"Eddie, try to get Babba's attention. I really need to talk to her about Christmas and it's me she's ignoring. She always likes talking to you."

"Pretend to argue with me," he said.

"What?"

"Come on, Madelyn, you know Babba. She can't stand having an argument going on and not being part of it. Start gesturing and looking mad, and pretend you're talking."

They must have been realistic because it took only thirty seconds for Babba to remove her headset, her eyes inquisitive.

Madelyn turned to her, making her voice serious. "Eddie's living with me," she told Babba, hoping that would shock her enough for her to leave the headset off. Eddie took her hand, as though offering support.

But "I figured he was" was all Babba said. Still, the headset stayed off.

Madelyn took a deep breath. "There's something else: he just got out of prison."

Babba's eyes positively danced with delight. "Were you in for political reasons?" she asked him.

Madelyn sighed. "Babba, this isn't Central America."

"I robbed a bank," Eddie said.

"I hope it was Chase Manhattan," said Babba, being flippant when Madelyn desperately wanted her to be serious.

"Babba, I didn't bring this up so that you and Eddie could discuss bank robberies. I really need your help."

Babba looked disgruntled that she wasn't going to get the conversation she had anticipated. She looked at Eddie, but Eddie just shrugged and said, "This is news to me, too."

"The thing is, Babba, the folks didn't know about Eddie, and then one morning Mom came by and caught him there; anyway, the upshot is, Eddie's spending Christmas with us."

Babba gave her a mischievous look. "I'll bet *that* set Shirley back on her heels."

"We convinced her it was innocent."

"You wouldn't convince *me* of that."

"I wouldn't try, Babba."

"You'll get a good meal, Eddie," said Babba. "Shirley always gets it catered."

"She does not," Madelyn said. "You know very well Mother's a good cook."

"Didn't learn it from me," Babba grumbled.

"If you'd just let me explain," Madelyn said. When no one interrupted, she went on. "They don't know about Eddie. They don't know he was in prison or how we met or anything."

"How did you meet?" Babba wanted to know.

"That's beside the point—"

"We corresponded," Eddie replied.

"Well, that's fine," Babba said. "Writing to prisoners is a family tradition, Madelyn. I think you know that."

Not wanting to get into Babba's recollections of all the anarchist friends she had known who ended up behind bars, Madelyn said, "Mom and Dad are going to question him like mad, come on as the heavy parents, and I just wish you'd be there for support. I don't think Eddie should have to come up against them on his own."

"Won't you be there?" asked Babba.

"Of course I'll be there, but they never pay any attention to me. Anyway, if you were to show up for your first Christmas with the family they would have something else to talk about."

Babba, who was far from stupid, said, "And, of course, you expect me to defend convicts in general and Eddie in particular."

"I don't need defending," said Eddie. "In fact, if it weren't for the fact that I'd love to have Christmas with you, Babba, I'd tell you to forget it."

Babba looked inordinately pleased by this.

"Please, Babba," said Madelyn, thinking that at least she hadn't said no outright.

"Will your father's people be there?"

"You know they will."

"And that snotty cousin of yours? What's her name?"

"Suzanna. Yes, she'll be there." And she could just imagine Suzanna's face when she showed up with Eddie.

"And her baby?"

"Yes, Babba, they'll all be there. But he's not a baby anymore."

"I will not bring gifts, nor do I wish to receive any."

Madelyn tried to keep the elation off her face. It had been easier than she had thought it would be. Although she knew by now what a soft spot Babba had for Eddie.

Babba, looking as though it had been she who put one over on Madelyn rather than the other way around, changed the subject. Madelyn figured she had a surprise in store for them, but she didn't even ask what it was. As long as she came, that was the important thing.

For the next hour Babba questioned Eddie on prison conditions, which Madelyn also found pretty interesting, since it was something Eddie never talked about. For her own part, she didn't bring it up because she hated to think of someone as good as Eddie having to be in a place like that. She watched them and listened and thought how nice it was that the two people she loved most in the world liked each other so much.

It might make it easier to face the disapproval her parents were sure to show. To say nothing of her father's parents and snotty Suzanna.

MADELYN WAS CHANGING and Eddie knew he had something to do with that change and he was glad of it. Gradually, from being compulsive about neatness, she was getting to where the bed seldom got made, and not only were coats left on chairs, sometimes clothes were strewn around the apartment.

Sex, of course, had a lot to do with it. From two people who had circled each other warily, seldom touching, they appeared to be bringing out the affectionate nature in each other, which neither of them had known they had before. Eddie couldn't remember getting or giving any affection as a child, and certainly there had been none in prison. And while he didn't know for sure, he had a feeling Madelyn had also lacked affection as a child. Even Babba, whom Madelyn dearly loved, was miserly in her displays of affection, and he would consider them verbal displays rather than physical.

Despite the fact that Madelyn would have been just as happy never to leave the apartment, the approach of Christmas forced them out. She had Christmas shopping to do, and then, as long as they had to shop anyway, she wanted to show him the store windows on Fifth Avenue and the tree in Rockefeller Center. He would have enjoyed those trips more if the streets and stores hadn't been so crowded with shoppers.

He wanted to get Madelyn a Christmas present and he wanted it to be perfect. It couldn't be clothes, because he didn't know the first thing about women's clothing and he didn't want to ask her what she liked because he wanted to surprise her. Toys came to mind, or at least games. But by now they had already bought just about every game that appealed to them, and really big games, things like pool tables or Ping-Pong tables, were too expensive, and she didn't have room for them in her apartment anyway.

So naturally he thought of jewelry. It was personal, it was something from him she could wear, and it was the kind of thing he knew men gave to women. Especially women they loved.

On his own one day, while Madelyn went on ahead to Babba's, he stopped in a jewelry store on Eighth Street and saw a fat, lopsided gold heart on a chain that he thought would be perfect. Sure, hearts were corny, but then so was love. And there was something humorous and yet touching about the shape of the heart. He had them gift-wrap it, then he hid it in the bottom of his athletic bag in the closet when he got home.

When it came time to buy a Christmas tree and decorate it, Madelyn also insisted on buying red stockings to hang up, telling him at the same time that he didn't have to fill hers with presents, that candy and fruit would do. So he bought Christmas candy and also a new deck of cards, since they had already worn the old one out, some plastic hair clips for her hair and two paperback books, and with the gold heart at the very bottom of her stocking, he managed to fill the whole thing.

He made the mistake of telling her that he had never had a real Christmas as a child. Madelyn had been planning on taking him to Washington Square Park on Christmas Eve to sing Christmas carols, but when she heard that, she changed her mind.

"We'll stay home and pretend we're children and Santa Claus is coming," she told him.

"Madelyn, I'm not a child."

"Well, for one night you're going to be."

She really went all out for Christmas. There was a big wreath on the front door, on the inside, not on the outside, because she said someone would steal it if she left it outside. She also bought pine branches and had arranged them on top of the bookcase. A poinsettia was in the center of the table, which also had a red tablecloth with reindeer on it. Red candles were set between the plants on the windowsills. And it seemed as if every day she was baking more Christmas cookies, which they usually ate before they were even cool.

Eddie couldn't remember ever knowing anyone who made such a fuss over Christmas. In the foster homes he had lived in there was never enough money for a real Christmas. A couple of times he could remember small, artificial trees, and sometimes he had been given articles of clothing. The clothing had always been used, though.

Christmas had been better in reform school, but the kids had always been so concerned with acting tough and cool that they mostly ignored any attempts by the school personnel to get them into the holiday spirit.

Christmas in prison had been ghastly. Most of the prisoners had wives or family of some kind on the outside, and despite the fact that many of them had visitors on Christmas, most of them became depressed during the holidays. There were more suicide attempts at that time of year than at any other.

He managed to avoid depression because Christmas had never meant anything to him anyway. On his own he would have just ignored the entire season this year, but it meant so much to Madelyn he felt he had to humor her. Anyway, whatever made Madelyn happy made him happy.

On Christmas Eve, as soon as they had finished dinner and cleaned up, Madelyn turned on the radio to a station that was playing Christmas music, then asked him to turn on the Christmas tree lights while she got a bag out of the closet. Inside were two red nightshirts with sprigs of holly sewn on the pockets, which she insisted they put on. Then she made them both eggnog and they sat down on the couch and Madelyn read him "A Visit from St. Nicholas" while he tried very hard to get into the mood. Her voice was lilting and childlike, and he enjoyed listening to it even if he found the poem rather boring. In fact, she had her hair pulled back with a red ribbon for the occasion, and she looked rather like a child as she sat in her nightshirt with her legs curled under her.

"How was that?" she asked him when she was finished.

"I know what would improve it."

"What?"

"Something stronger in the eggnog."

"Eddie, we're supposed to be children."

He reached over and pulled her toward him, but she pushed his hand away and straightened up. "I'm not finished."

"You are so, 'Merry Christmas to all and to all a good night' is the end, isn't it?"

But she just gave him a mysterious look and got up and took another book off the shelf. "You're really going to love this one," she promised.

And he did. It was *The Grinch Who Stole Christmas* and he found it pretty entertaining. When she finished reading, it was still only eight o'clock. He just hoped she didn't go in for Dickens.

"You liked *that* one, didn't you?" she asked.

"Yeah, it was great. What're you going to read next?"

"That's it."

"So what do we do now?"

"Well, when I was a kid, that's when I had to go to bed."

He grinned. "Great!"

"But I don't feel like going to bed this early."

"Sure you do," he coaxed.

"Eddie, that wouldn't be right. We're supposed to be children."

"That was your idea, not mine. Why don't we grow up for the rest of the night?"

He could tell she was tempted. "Not yet. It's too early."

"We could empty our stockings."

She looked shocked. "Not until tomorrow morning, Eddie. Santa Claus hasn't come yet."

He gave a pointed look in the direction of the bulging stockings, which were held by thumbtacks to the bookcase.

"Don't be so literal. You've got to pretend."

"I'm not very good at pretending," he admitted, which was the truth. God knows he had tried hard enough in prison at times, but it had never worked.

"I'm good enough at pretending for both of us."

"All right, then what do we do now?"

"I guess we should have gone caroling." She gave him a beseeching look. "Do you know any Christmas carols?"

"Madelyn, I'm not sitting around here singing."

"You know what we should do, Eddie?"

"As long as we don't have to get dressed and go out." It wasn't going to snow for Christmas, but the temperature had dropped and he could hear the wind whistling around the building.

"We should write each other a Christmas letter to put in the stockings. I've missed getting your letters."

He put an arm around her and pulled her close. "You mean you wouldn't rather have me in person?"

"You know I don't mean that. But I loved writing to you."

"Yeah, I liked it, too. Okay, I kind of like that idea."

Madelyn got them each some notebook paper and a pen, then she went up to her loft bed for privacy. Eddie sat for a while, trying to put his thoughts into words, then started writing.

FOR MADELYN, WRITING had always been easier than speaking. She was sure Eddie knew how she felt about him, but she had never actually put it into words. Now, on paper, she felt she could.

Dear Eddie,

I want you to know first of all that this is the very best time I've ever had in my life, and the very, very best Christmas.

I never realized how nice it would be to have someone around all the time. I never had any brothers or sisters to talk to or play with and my parents never did anything but work, and then, when they were home, talk about work. I was always happiest by myself just reading and, for a time, writing you letters.

Now I know what I was missing. I just love being able to talk to you whenever I want, and you always listen to me. And I love having someone to cook for and to eat with and to do the shopping with me.

And of course I love going to bed with you, but you know that. I'm not just talking about sex, either. I love to go to sleep with your body curled around mine and wake up in the morning with you next to me.

I'm so glad I answered that ad of yours. I think it must have been fate, don't you? I wonder if I hadn't met you that way whether we would have met some other way. Sometimes I think about that.

I imagine you know I love you. I've never been in love before and I never will be again, because I'm going to love you forever. I've heard people say they've found their other half and I never understood it before, but now I do. Because you're my other half.

I don't want you to worry about what my parents think of you because that doesn't matter to me in the least. Once they get to know you, if they don't love you and respect you the way I do, well, that's their problem, not ours. I think, though, that maybe they'll be happy for me. I hope so. But even if they aren't, I'm happy enough myself that it doesn't matter.

I want this to be the best Christmas you ever had. And this is all I'm going to write because already I miss you and want you to come up here with me. Playing at being children was fun, but now I would rather be adults again, if you know what I mean. Merry Christmas, Eddie.

All my love,
Madelyn

"Eddie?" she called.

"Yeah?"

"You finished yet?"

"Not yet."

Madelyn leaned over the side of the loft bed and looked down. He was writing away. "Are you *almost* finished?"

"You didn't tell me there was a time limit to this."

"There isn't but I'm finished."

"So write some more."

"I've said everything I wanted to say."

He looked up at her, his eyes gleaming. "Are we still children?"

"Why don't you come up and find out?"

He gave her a teasing look. "No, I feel like writing some more."

"Eddie!"

He laughed. "You've got to learn to have a little patience, Madelyn."

"If you don't come up here, I'm coming down there."

"This was your idea. Now let me finish. Just pretend I'm still in prison and not down here."

Fuming, she lay back on the bed and crossed her arms.

The bank was decorated for Christmas. There was a tree by the door with presents wrapped in gold foil beneath it. Poinsettias were arranged on all the desks and along the counter in front of the teller's cages.

The bank was crowded with people depositing their Christmas bonuses and withdrawing money for the holidays. There was a long line, and nearly every customer was carrying a shopping bag filled with Christmas purchases.

When Madelyn finally got up to the counter, she noticed that all the tellers were wearing Christmas corsages and they were saying "Have a happy holiday" instead of "Have a nice day," which she thought was an improvement. She didn't like being told to have a nice day. It always sounded like an order.

Her teller was a young woman who still smiled at her even though it had probably been a long, busy day. "Can I help you?" she asked Madelyn.

Madelyn smiled back. "Yes, you certainly can." She got an envelope out of her handbag, one with a Christmas card inside, and slipped it through to the teller. "I'd like you to put five hundred dollars in that envelope. That's all I want, in hundreds, please. If you do this, no one will get hurt."

The teller was looking confused. "May I have your passbook, please?" she finally asked.

Madelyn, still smiling, shook her head. "I'm afraid not. I don't have an account here. I do have a gun, however, but I'd rather not have to use it this close to Christmas. Now just do as I say and don't press any buttons or signal anyone. Surely the bank can afford to be robbed of five hundred dollars."

At the word "robbed," the woman's eyes widened and she nervously licked her lips. "Yes, ma'am just keep calm."

"I'm perfectly calm," Madelyn informed her.

She watched as the teller counted out five crisp hundred-dollar bills, then slipped them inside the envelope. Her eyes still wide, she pushed the envelope out to Madelyn.

"That was very good," Madelyn told her. "Now I want you to just behave normally until you see me get out the door. Then feel free to do whatever you want. Do you understand?"

The teller nodded.

"Fine. Have a nice holiday," said Madelyn, turning around and walking slowly to the door of the bank. She pushed open the glass door, then quickly mingled with the crowds of people on Thirty-fourth Street. In less than a minute she was across the street and on the escalator in Macy's. As long as she was there, she might as well go to the fifth floor and buy some new luggage. There were a lot of things she wanted to take with her to South America.

"Madelyn?"

She opened her eyes and came back to reality. "What is it, Eddie?"

"I'm finished," he called up to her.

"That's nice."

A silence, then, "What're you doing up there?"

"Just thinking about Christmas."

"Want some company?"

She leaned over the side and grinned at him. "Have a nice holiday, Eddie."

"What's that supposed to mean?"

"Come on up and find out."

Just his climbing into bed with her seemed to raise the room temperature by ten degrees. She lay naked under the covers, having converted to his way of thinking that wearing clothes of any kind in bed was superfluous, particularly since they would sooner or later be removed.

Anyway, she loved the feel of his warm body against hers. She, who had always sworn by down comforters, now needed no more than Eddie beside her to sleep in peaceful warmth.

Side by side, their arms around each other, he entered her, not in passion this time, but with the feeling that being connected that way was the natural extension of all the other ways they now were connected. She wrapped her leg around him, pulling herself in closer, letting her mind relax and her feelings take over. And, as it had ever since the second time they had made love, this worked the magic.

She could feel the tension in her body building up, reaching one plateau and hovering there for a while before suddenly moving up higher, then higher, and without thinking about it, her body knowing it would keep going up and up until there was nowhere farther to go and then, reaching the summit and losing all conscious thought at all, just knowing, knowing in every cell of her body, that what was happening was a miracle and not to be explained, but that it was her miracle, hers and Eddie's.

And when later he said, "Wasn't that better than a letter?" all she could do was silently nod as she clung to him, and wonder at her stupidity when he first arrived and she had mourned the fact their letter-writing days were over.

Writing letters had never made her feel like this.

Chapter Eight

She found she really was as excited as a kid.

It was barely light out when Madelyn woke up. Eddie stirred but didn't wake as she climbed over him and went down the ladder. She turned the radio on so that Christmas music was playing softly, then plugged in the lights to the tree.

She measured out coffee into the coffee maker and turned on the oven to warm the croissants. She cooked a batch of scrambled eggs, then got everything ready on the table. Only then did she call up to Eddie.

"Wake up, Eddie. Merry Christmas."

She heard a groan; then he said, "It's not even light out yet."

"I swear, Eddie, you were never a child. Come on, you got plenty of sleep." Then she remembered that while they had gone to bed early, that hadn't meant they'd had plenty of sleep.

He was climbing down the ladder, his muscular legs sticking out the bottom of the nightshirt. She went to him and hugged him, loving the way his arms just naturally went around her, the way he looked in the morning with his hair falling over his forehead.

"This is nice," he said, looking at the food and the lighted candles she had placed on the table.

"You want orange juice?"

He shook his head. "Just coffee."

"After breakfast we'll empty our stockings and read our letters."

"And then what do we do until it's time to leave for your parents' place?"

She grinned at him. "Play with our toys."

"I hope you didn't get me an electric train or something."

"No, but I thought about it."

He laughed, then dug into his eggs.

Madelyn split open one of the croissants with a knife and filled it with scrambled eggs. She could hardly wait to get to the stockings. It wasn't the gifts she was interested in but the letter. Then she had the horrible thought that maybe his would be impersonal and hers would end up embarrassing them both.

But no, there was nothing to be embarrassed about. Eddie loved her and she loved him, and surely they could say whatever they wanted to each other without being embarrassed. Anyway, he had already told her he loved her; she was the one who had never voiced it.

When they were finished, she just stacked the dishes in the sink, then went and took down both stockings. She handed him his; then they went over and sat crosslegged on the rug, facing each other.

She took out his letter and put it aside for last and reached in and exclaimed over the small gifts and candy. Then, at the bottom, she felt a box and pulled it out. She carefully undid the ribbon and paper, then opened it and looked at the gold heart.

She felt tears in her eyes as she looked at Eddie. He was watching her and she could tell he wasn't sure she would like it. "Oh, Eddie," she said. "It's so perfect. So lovely."

"You really like it?"

"I *love* it. I'll put it on and never take it off."

He seemed to relax. "Put it on now. Let me see it on you."

She fastened the chain around her neck, then looked down at the gleaming heart against her nightshirt.

"Merry Christmas," he said, leaning over and kissing her.

She had put only candy and fruit in his stocking, and now she got up and went to the closet where she had put the presents she had bought for everyone. She pulled out three large boxes and brought them over to him.

"That's too much," said Eddie, looking at them.

"No, it's not, and none is as nice as what you gave me. It's just stuff I thought you needed."

He opened them up, ripping off the wrapping paper. There was a down-filled, hooded parka in navy blue, which he really needed in the cold. There were also a pair of charcoal-gray wool slacks, a red wool shirt, a plaid muffler and a pair of leather gloves. She was hoping he would wear the new clothes to her parents' place for dinner, but she would never suggest it to him. She just knew how dressed up everyone would be and would hate for him to feel out of place.

He was feeling the clothes, not saying anything, and she asked, "Do you like them? You can always return them if you don't."

"Of course I like them. It's just too much, Madelyn."

"I thought maybe you were tired of wearing my clothes." She had some sweatshirts and sweatpants that fit him, and he wore them around the house most of the time.

He reached over and took her hand. "When I get a job, I'll make it up to you."

"There's nothing to make up, Eddie." To stop any further conversation on the subject, she unfolded his letter to her and began to read it, seeing out of the corner of her eye that he was doing the same.

Dear Madelyn,

For the first time in my life I feel like a worthwhile human being, and it's all because of you. You have shown me what love is, what caring for another person is, what a home is, and most of all, what it feels like to have someone's respect.

I knew from your letters that you were a good person, but it wasn't until I met you that I knew how good. You took me in when I was really a stranger, an ex-con, and you never made me feel uneasy or like I didn't belong. You are beautiful and good and loving and generous and have given me all the things I never thought I would have with a woman.

I will tell you something that I never thought I would say: You made the ten years in prison worth it. I would gladly do it over if it meant knowing you at the end of it.

You have my love, all of it.

Eddie

Madelyn had never known that such happiness could be hers.

EDDIE WAS GLAD of the new clothes when he saw how dressed up Madelyn got. She wore a black velvet dress, and stockings and high heels, and she had even put her hair on top of her head and wore earrings. He thought maybe she was trying to look more adult for facing her parents. She also wore a black cape with a hood with fur around it.

He was glad of the new parka, because it was cold and windy when they went outside to get a taxi to pick up Babba. "You nervous?" Madelyn asked him.

"Not as nervous as you," he told her. He could tell by the way she held herself just how tense she was.

Babba was waiting for them in front of her building. She was bundled up in something that looked like a blanket, with only her eyes showing.

"Don't say Merry Christmas to her," Madelyn warned him before he got out and helped Babba into the taxi.

Madelyn reached over and gave Babba a kiss on the cheek, which was tolerated but not reciprocated. "I hope we don't have to stay there all night," said Babba.

"We'll get you home by eight, how's that?" Madelyn said.

Babba made a grumbling sound, but didn't demur. Eddie had a feeling she had on her Sony Walkman under the blanket and wasn't listening to them anyway.

Madelyn gave the driver an address Eddie didn't recognize and he said, "Where do your parents live?"

"SoHo."

He wasn't familiar with that area. "Is that where you grew up?"

"No, they had an apartment on the West Side. They moved to SoHo a couple of years ago. They bought a loft."

Eddie didn't know what a loft was exactly, but he guessed it would be easier just to wait and see. He had read about them and had a general idea they were old warehouses that had been converted into living space, but that didn't sound like the kind of thing her parents would have. He would have thought Fifth Avenue would be more their style.

The taxi pulled up to a building that didn't look like much to Eddie from the outside. Inside there wasn't a lobby or doorman or anything, just an elevator. They got in in silence, Madelyn clutching his hand. She pressed the button for the top floor, and what really surprised him was that when they got there, there was an iron grate over the door and beyond was the loft. That made him understand they had the entire floor.

Madelyn's father came to unlock the grate, which slid back, and then Eddie was looking in amazement at the most enormous living room he had ever seen.

He thought it could easily have held a regulation bas-
ketball court.

"It looks like a museum, doesn't it?" murmured
Madelyn, taking off her cape and handing it to the
maid who appeared.

The walls were white and the floors of bare wood,
except for a few rugs that were thick and fluffy. Very
modern, colorful paintings were displayed, and the
furniture was all sleek with straight lines. A white
Christmas tree, at least eight feet tall, stood in one
corner, and all the decorations were made of spar-
kling crystal.

Babba removed her blanket and Eddie saw she was
wearing a red velour jogging outfit. It made her look
like a Christmas elf. The Walkman had been left
home, apparently, and in its place was a red head-
band.

Mr. Shaffer looked ill at ease, but his wife came up
to them and gave Madelyn a hug, saying, "Merry
Christmas, darling." Then she leaned down to give
Babba a kiss on the cheek. Babba stiffened visibly and
didn't say a word when Madelyn's mother said, "I'm
so glad you came, Mother."

Then she turned to Eddie and held out her hand. He
took it, thinking how lovely she looked in her long
skirt and ruffled blouse, her face not looking much
older than Madelyn's. Eddie said, "Thank you for
inviting me."

Then Eddie was led into the room by Mrs. Shaffer
and introduced to Mr. Shaffer's parents, whose short,
fluffy gray hair and pink faces made them look like

twins, except that Mr. Shaffer was thin and Mrs. Shaffer was plump.

Then he was introduced to Madelyn's cousin Suzanna, a flamboyant blonde of about twenty-five, who was holding a small boy by the hand. He saw Madelyn bend down to pick up her little cousin and he discerned that even though she might not like "snotty Suzanna," she certainly was crazy about the child.

Eddie realized how clever Madelyn had been in inducing Babba to come, because everyone was making a big fuss over her, which left him out of the limelight. He could see that Babba hated every minute of it, and he loved her for doing it for him.

He was handed a cup of eggnog, this time liberally dosed with something strong, and he took a seat beside Madelyn on one of the several couches. Then he noticed the grand piano in one corner, hardly taking up any of the floor space.

There was some general conversation about the weather, some mention of Suzanna's parents being in Jamaica for Christmas, and then Suzanna's husband came out of one of the rooms Eddie hadn't seen and was introduced to him. He was about Eddie's age and he tried to engage Eddie in talk of the Super Bowl that was coming up, but Eddie hadn't followed football that year and didn't have anything to say.

Babba caught Eddie's eye and winked at him before launching into a lengthy diatribe about apartheid in South Africa, in an attempt, he felt, to keep the conversation from moving on to him.

Everyone listened politely except for Shirley Shaffer, who excused herself to go to the kitchen. No one, however, appeared to be in agreement with Babba, with the possible exception of Madelyn, and she was keeping her mouth shut. Eddie didn't know much about South Africa and kept Babba going by asking questions, but it was clearly a matter of time before Babba was going to run out of things to say.

He should've known Babba had other resources at hand. She started in by asking her son-in-law about the loft, which launched him into a long story about the deal they made on it, and all the improvements they had made, and how much it was worth on to-day's market—all of which Eddie found pretty bor-ing but he listened attentively nonetheless.

He had to admit, though, that he was impressed by Madelyn's parents. They were both good-looking, in-telligent, well-spoken and successful, and he couldn't imagine not being proud of them as parents. In fact, he envied Madelyn her whole family. If he had had just one relative, it would have meant a lot to him. Even though there were undercurrents of dissent within the family, all in all, being part of such a group, even temporarily, gave him a warm feeling. He loved Madelyn all for herself, but he was also ready to love her entire family.

Babba he was already crazy about, and he liked her even more when she said to Suzanna, "You play the piano, don't you? Why don't you play something for us?"

He saw Suzanna shoot Babba a poisonous look, but then the elderly Shaffers asked her, too, and with a great show of reluctance she got up and walked over to the piano. She began playing "White Christmas" loudly and not well, and soon everyone got up and walked over to the piano to sing to her accompaniment.

Eddie was finally pulled up from the couch by Madelyn, but he saw that Babba was standing her ground and not joining in. She seemed determined not to give in to the holiday spirit.

They were on "Jingle Bells" when Shirley came back into the room and announced that dinner was ready. Suzanna didn't even finish the song. She just got up and said, "It's about time," under her breath, causing Madelyn to laugh.

"Better you than me," Madelyn said to her.

Suzanna gave her a rueful look. "I can remember the days when you accompanied me on the violin."

"You play the violin?" Eddie asked her.

"Not since high school. And never well. Try as we might, no one in the family really has any musical talent. Except Babba, but she never played for the family."

The dining room had a table that would have seated half his cell block. Mr. Shaffer gave a little speech about how happy it made him to have the family around him at Christmas, and then the food was served. Eddie had never seen so much at one table. He helped himself to a little of everything and figured the worst was over, that no one would be able to talk with so much food to eat, but he was mistaken.

Dinner conversation seemed to be required. After the general comments about how good the food looked and tasted, it got to question-and-answer time.

Suzanna's husband, Steve, was asked how things were going in his neck of the woods, and it turned out he was a doctor and the conversation briefly touched on plastic surgery, with Steve offering to give free face-lifts to everyone present. None of them took him up on it and Eddie had the feeling this was an inside joke.

Suzanna talked about how hard it was to find a good nursery school, and Madelyn kept this going by asking her questions about the various nursery schools Suzanna had been to. Eddie had the feeling Madelyn was genuinely interested and not just making small talk.

Inevitably, though, the conversation finally turned to him. It was Madelyn's paternal grandmother, oddly enough, who initiated it. Eddie had been sure it would come from Madelyn's mother. The old lady quite innocently asked Madelyn how she and Eddie had met, and then there was dead silence around the table as all eyes shifted to Madelyn.

Eddie could tell Madelyn was stunned, although she should have been expecting the inquiry. He looked at her and saw that she was trying to think up something acceptable to say and nothing was coming to mind. Not wanting to put her in the kind of position where she felt she had to lie for him, he answered for her.

He said calmly, "Madelyn and I met when I was released from prison. We had been pen pals for three years before that."

There was the silence of held breath for about ten seconds, and then Babba chimed in with, "It's so comforting to know that the art of letter writing has

not been lost. Too many people today rely on the telephone. Of course *I* don't.''

No one took up telephones as a valid conversa-
tional gambit. Eddie looked at Madelyn's mother and
saw she was in a state of shock. Her father didn't look
much better. Then Eddie caught Suzanna's eye across
the table. The young woman was looking at him as
though he had been stripped naked and she found him
sexy.

He felt everyone was waiting for him to say something more, but he couldn't think of anything to say.
He had a feeling they wouldn't be quite as fascinated
by his bank robbery as Madelyn had been.

Steve asked him which prison he had been in and
Eddie told him, and again there was silence.

Then Suzanna said, ''Well, really, everyone is
looking as though the Boston Strangler were sitting
down to dinner with us.'' She appeared to be viewing
Madelyn with new respect. ''I, for one, think it's
pretty exciting. No stuffy dentists or accountants for
our Madelyn. You've turned out to be quite a dark
horse, Cousin.''

He took Madelyn's hand beneath the table and felt
how cold it was. ''Actually, I'm planning to be an ac-
countant,'' he said to Suzanna. ''Sorry to disappoint
you.''

Babba gave a very loud sigh, a really melodramatic
one that drew the attention to herself. ''They're too
polite to ask you, Eddie, so I'm going to set them
straight before they get the idea you committed some
unmentionable crime. He robbed a bank when he was
a teenager, that's all. And I don't think I have to point

out that he's ten years older and at least that much wiser by now. So you don't have to lock up your jewelry, Shirley.''

Shirley turned red, making Eddie think she had been thinking of doing just that.

''A *bank* robber,'' breathed Suzanna, who seemed to find it every bit as romantic as Madelyn. ''You certainly make our family sound dull by comparison.''

And then Babba brought down the house. ''Oh, I don't know,'' she said, her eyes throwing off sparks. ''Shirley's father spent some years in prison. Inciting to riot was the charge, and then they found he had also been making bombs in his basement.''

The next sound was Shirley's crystal goblet crashing down on her plate.

MADELYN REMEMBERED the rest of the day in bits and snatches.

Babba's announcement about Shirley's father had been a terrible shock to Madelyn's mother. To Madelyn's knowledge, Shirley had never been told anything about him, although she knew she was illegitimate and had grown up feeling humiliated by this fact. Madelyn's father had known about it, but Madelyn didn't think anyone else in the family had been let in on the secret, despite the fact that being illegitimate no longer was the stigma it had once been.

Madelyn knew that Babba had spilled the secret about Shirley's father for Eddie's sake, and she loved her for it, but she didn't want to see her mother hurt just to protect Eddie. She didn't think Eddie needed that kind of protection.

Still, there was no shutting up Babba when she wanted to say something or shock somebody. And she had clearly wanted to shock her daughter out of her middle-class complacency. It didn't matter that Shirley's father had been jailed for political reasons; to Shirley, that was every bit as bad as having been jailed as a common criminal.

Still, Madelyn thought that anyone with any brains at all would have figured Shirley's father to have been an anarchist like Babba. Madelyn was sure that those were the kind of people Babba had always associated with. If Shirley had had some dream of a father who was like herself, then she had been very wrong.

After she dropped her water goblet and it smashed against her plate, Shirley had rushed from the room, and seconds later her husband had followed her.

Everyone at the table seemed to be embarrassed except Babba. Even Suzanna turned horror-stricken eyes to Madelyn. And Eddie had said to Babba, "That really wasn't necessary."

Babba's eyes had been piercing as she looked at Eddie. "Oh, yes, it was, young man. The whole family would be nice and polite about your prison record because they're always nice and polite at the dinner table. But there would have been plenty of talk afterward, in private, and it wouldn't have been so nice and polite. I just wanted to point out that every family has someone who's broken the law, whether they've been caught or not. You've served your time, Eddie, and that's quite enough punishment."

Then, in an unprecedented gesture toward her daughter, Babba stood up and excused herself. "I think it's about time Shirley heard about her father," she remarked, and then went off to find her daughter.

Madelyn's other grandmother, who was always good in bad situations, called for the maid to clear the table, then supervised the serving of the dessert.

At some point after the meal was finished, Suzanna cornered her and said, "Personally, I find it exciting and romantic. I like your Eddie. You two living together?"

Madelyn nodded. She was tired of telling lies.

"You going to get married or what?"

"I don't know; we haven't talked about it. Eddie's going to have to find a job and then get registered to finish college."

Suzanna looked a trifle disappointed, as though she had expected him to continue in his career as a bank robber. "Well, listen, Madelyn, if you ever need someone to talk to, give me a call."

It was a day of surprises. Never before had Suzanna expressed any interest in talking with Madelyn. Despite the fact that Madelyn was several years older than her cousin, Suzanna had always seemed far more sophisticated and self-assured.

Her grandfather got her aside and told her he liked her young man and that he had been in trouble once when he was a youth, too.

"Oh, Grandpa, I don't believe that for a minute. But it's sweet of you to say so."

The old man looked chagrined. "Well, it wasn't anything like robbing a bank, but I did steal some of my mother's housekeeping money out of the jar she kept it in. Got a whipping for it, too."

Madelyn gave him a hug, thinking it was turning out to be a day for confessions.

Madelyn saw her father come out of the master bedroom; then, about twenty minutes later, Babba came out. When Shirley didn't appear, Madelyn went in to see her.

It was the first time she had ever seen her mother cry. Shirley was sitting on the velvet chaise longue and mascara was smeared on her cheeks. Madelyn sat down beside her and put her arm around her.

"I'm sorry Babba said that. She could've done it in private."

"Since when has my mother ever done *any*thing in private? Next it will probably appear in the Letters to the Editor in the *Times*."

That made Madelyn smile. "I guess she was afraid you'd disapprove of Eddie for me."

"Well, of course I disapprove of him. Ask the mother of any one of your friends if she'd like to see her daughter living with a former convict and see what reaction you'd get. But he does seem nice and well-mannered, and it's clear to anyone that he cares for you. Anyway, it's not Eddie I'm upset about."

"She'd never told you about your father, had she?"

Shirley shook her head. "No, she always gave me the idea she set out to have a love child and the father was of no importance. Now I find out he was in jail when I was born, and after that they had political differences and she refused to marry him just to give me a last name."

"Does it really matter after all this time?"

Shirley gave Madelyn a strange look. "Yes, it does. What's more, she just told me that my father is not only alive, he still lives in New York."

"I have another grandfather?"

"That's right. I'm surprised she didn't bring *him* to dinner, too."

"Are you going to look him up?"

For the first time, Shirley looked defenseless and in danger of falling apart. "I just might. He couldn't be any worse than my mother."

"I love Babba."

"I know you do. Of course you do; she's an interesting, eccentric grandmother. But you didn't have to grow up with her. Would you have liked a mother who made political speeches at PTA meetings? Who was standing outside the movie theater getting people to sign petitions when you came out of the movie with your date? Who never dressed or acted like any of your friends' mothers? I know it sounds humorous now, but it's not funny when you're a child and trying to be accepted."

Madelyn didn't know what to say to that. She hadn't thought her own mother was perfect, but at least she had never been embarrassed by her.

Before the gathering broke up, her father took her aside. "Is your young man looking for a job?"

She nodded. "I've been telling him if he worked for one of the universities he'd get free tuition, so I think he's going to look into that."

"Sounds like a smart idea. I just wanted to say, honey, that if he should need some kind of letter of recommendation, I'd be glad to give him one."

At least he hadn't offered Eddie a job. She would hate to see Eddie working for her father. "Thanks, Dad, he'll appreciate that."

"No one's going to hold his past against him, Maddy."

"He had a rough childhood, in and out of foster homes."

"All I need to know, Maddy, is that he's good to you. And anyone can see he's crazy about you."

"I feel the same about him."

"Well, good. Be pretty interesting to hear about that bank robbery of his sometime. Not today, of course, with everyone around."

Madelyn smiled. "Get him to tell you, it's a pretty funny story."

LATER IN THE TAXI, as she was taking Babba home, Madelyn said, "I hear I have a grandfather in New York."

Babba grunted.

"I'd like to meet him," Madelyn persisted.

"He lives two doors down from me," said Babba.

"You mean you still see him?"

"I see him around, but we don't speak. He's a *socialist*," she said, as though that explained it all.

"Did you tell Mom that?"

Babba chuckled. "No, I thought I'd let her find out for herself."

To Madelyn's mother, socialism was every bit as unacceptable as anarchism.

When they got home, Madelyn said, "I want to apologize, Eddie. You probably never expected anything like that."

"I enjoyed myself," said Eddie.

"You're *kidding*!"

"I like your family. It was nice spending Christmas with a family."

"Nice?"

"You have a pretty interesting family."

"Well, to tell you the truth, they did seem more human today. I even liked Suzanna."

"Cute litte boy she has."

"Yes, Brian's a sweetie. She drops him off and lets me baby-sit for him sometimes."

"Lets you?"

"Oh, Eddie, I don't mind. I know she's using me. But it's about the only way I ever get to see him."

"Are you going to meet your grandfather?"

"Of course. Want to come with me?"

"I wouldn't miss it for the world."

"Imagine living two doors away from each other and never speaking. Wouldn't it be something if they got together again?"

"It's been a lot of years."

"Maybe we could get them together."

Eddie put his arms around her. "You're a hopeless romantic, you know that?"

She knew it and what's more, she thought, Eddie's being there was living proof.

Chapter Nine

Once he had the full realization, Eddie knew it had been a gradual process. There had been small clues, sometimes a sense of déjà vu. There had been times he had sensed it without actually defining what he was sensing.

The fact was, it finally dawned on him that the life Madelyn had constructed for him was, in its way, every bit as confining as a prison. In fact it was a prison, albeit not one controlled by the state.

The cell might have all the comforts of home, the warden might be loving and eager to fulfill his needs, but he was as much a prisoner as he had been in the state penitentiary.

There was a word for ex-convicts who constructed a life for themselves on the outside along the lines of a prison. The word was "institutionalized." These were the ones who couldn't handle freedom. No matter how often they did time and were released, they couldn't be sprung mentally. Once free, they longed to return to the security of confinement, where their existence was defined. If they didn't actually aspire to return to a real prison, they made their own. The thing was, Eddie didn't think he would have been like this on his own. But he had certainly not tried to stop Madelyn from turning her apartment into a cozy cell.

He didn't think she was even aware of it. He knew her to be naturally reclusive and he had joined in as her willing accomplice. He realized that every time he suggested they go out to do something, she always had an excuse. Usually it was the weather, and true enough, it had been a cold December. He was certain, though, that had the weather been balmy, she would've come up with some other excuse. And when she looked at him with her eyes wide and said, "But wouldn't you rather stay home? Just the two of us? We can have just as much fun here," he could never refuse her.

At first he hadn't even wanted to. He had never been so happy, had never loved anyone before. Of course, he was content to be alone with her. But he came to realize on their infrequent forays out that he enjoyed the city streets, that he looked forward to getting to know the city.

He knew he should never have let her talk him into not looking for a job or his own place right away. Now his money had dwindled to just over a hundred dollars and he was an economic prisoner if nothing else. And there was also the knowledge that he was living off her. What was even worse, he was living off her parents. Living off anybody didn't appeal to him. He had always thought of himself as independent, and now he couldn't claim to be even partly independent.

He woke up on December 29 and realized that he was stifling. It had nothing to do with his love for Madelyn, other than that he felt if their present life-style continued it would do some irreparable damage to that love. He felt caged, and with that feeling there was a slight, but growing, resentment of Madelyn for caging him. He knew the feeling wasn't going to go away. He also knew it wasn't something he could discuss with Madelyn, not unless he wanted to hurt her, and that was about the last thing he wanted to do.

He also realized something else, and this pretty much surprised him. He was missing the companionship of males. Now, if anyone had asked him, he would have said that his fellow inmates had been a pretty sleazy bunch, not the kind of people he cared to see again. But that hadn't been true. Oh, sure, they had their share of sleazes, but he had also made some good friends in the joint. Guys he could talk to and kid around with, and who shared with him a sense of camaraderie. They didn't even come close to being to him what Madelyn was, but he missed being able to talk about things and say things that he would hesitate to talk about or say to her. All his life he had made male friends and he was beginning to miss that.

The male friends he wasn't worried about. He knew he'd meet plenty of guys either at school or on the job. It was just that he was beginning to wonder if he'd ever get a job or get into school. Madelyn didn't want to discuss either, would just tell him to wait until the first of the year. Well, the first of the year was just a few days off and he guessed he could wait if he had to, but he also didn't see any harm in at least walking over to

New York University to see what the job situation looked like.

There were other schools in the city he could try, but he liked the Village and wasn't looking to be too far away from Madelyn. He wanted both. He wanted Madelyn and he also wanted freedom. And he was awfully afraid she wasn't going to understand.

And then he began to feel guilty. He was awake and making escape plans, and Madelyn, who didn't deserve this, was asleep beside him, unaware that a traitor was sharing her bed. Asleep and looking innocent and sexy at the same time.

An irresistable combination.

NOW SHE WAS DREAMING bank robberies, this one in Technicolor. She was at the good part, the really exciting part, the part where she was making a deal with the cops who were surrounding the bank, which had to be a direct result of watching *Dog Day Afternoon* on television the night before, and she was really getting into it, really enjoying the dream, and then she came awake abruptly and saw Eddie leaning over her. He was naked, and she was about to complain because she wanted to finish the dream, but then he was kissing her and the dream began to fade and a blissful reality took its place. It was better than any dream she could have conceived. It was his flesh and her flesh joining, melding, and yet it went beyond mere flesh to become something magical.

"Wasn't that a great way to wake up?" he asked her afterward, and she wasn't sure she liked his smug tone.

She got her breathing under control and said, "I was having a good dream."

"About me?"

She tried to remember whether he had been in on the bank robbery, but she didn't think so. In fact, it was her recollection that she had been doing it alone. That was a first. She was progressing in her ability to rob banks, it seemed. "No, it wasn't about you."

"You mean you were dreaming about another man?"

"Eddie, my dreams rarely have men in them."

"That's pretty abnormal, Madelyn."

"I don't think it's abnormal at all. Actually, my dreams usually have something to do with whatever I was reading before I went to bed."

"You didn't read last night."

"I said *usually*."

"So what was this one about?"

"None of your business." Then she saw the surprised look on his face and said, "Eddie, don't I get any privacy?"

"I guess you don't get much with me around, do you?"

"As much as I want," she told him. She wondered for about the millionth time why she was being so secretive about her bank robbery fixation.

"I've been thinking," he said.

"Excellent."

"You know, you have a pretty smart mouth on you at times."

"Okay, what were you thinking?"

"I'm thinking I shouldn't go along with you when you meet your grandfather today."

"Oh, please, Eddie."

"No, I'm serious. It should be your mother who goes with you. After all, it's her father."

"She doesn't know about it."

"I know, and I think that's wrong. I think you ought to at least call her and tell her, see if she wants to go."

"You really think so?"

"Yeah, I really do. He's only your grandfather, but he's her father. She must have spent a lot of time wondering about him. I would've if it had been my father."

"Me, too." She would have done something her mother wouldn't have done, though; she would have romanticized him out of all proportion. "Okay, I'll call her. But if she doesn't want to go, won't you come with me?"

"No. I think it should be private. Family. Anyway, I've been thinking I might go over to NYU and check out the job situation."

"It's Christmas vacation."

"Sure, but the offices don't close down, do they?"

"I guess not."

"And it might be a good time because everyone else might be waiting for the first of the year."

She didn't want to think about him working or even going to school, but she knew his pride would eventually get in the way of things. She could tell every time she paid for groceries or anything else that it was bothering him. "Okay, Eddie," she said, trying to

sound happy about it and knowing she wasn't succeeding.

She got up and called her mother at work, but was
put on hold for a while; when her mother came on,
Madelyn said, not even trying to soften the shock of
it, "I'm going to meet my grandfather today and I
thought maybe you'd like to come along."

Her mother knew right away what grandfather she
meant. "Did my mother set this up?"

"No. She just told me his name and where he lived,
and I looked up his number in the phone book and
called him."

"I don't even know his name," said Shirley.

"It's Joseph. Joseph Mihalenko."

"What was that last name?"

Madelyn repeated it for her.

"What kind of name is that?"

"I don't know. I guess we can ask him."

"My God, I'm turning out to be some nationality I
didn't even know about."

"You're still the same person, Mom."

"I feel as if I don't know myself anymore."

"If you'd rather not meet him—"

"No, of course I want to meet him. What did he say
when you called him?"

"Not much. He knew about you but not about
me."

"Did he sound glad to hear from you?"

Madelyn couldn't remember him sounding any way
in particular. "Not really, but he invited me over."

"My father. And with a name I can't even spell."

"Well, look, Mom, I'm going over there at two o'clock. You want to meet me for lunch first?"

They made arrangements to meet at a Japanese restaurant near Madelyn's apartment; then she hung up and turned to Eddie.

"What kind of name do you think Mihalenko is?" she asked him.

He shrugged. "You got me. Maybe Russian, something like that."

"Mother will *die* if it's Russian."

Eddie was starting to grin. As always, he seemed amused and intrigued by her family. "That bad, huh? Your mom doesn't like Russians?"

"I don't know about the people; she sure hates their political system."

"He's probably a good Russian anarchist."

"Babba says he's a socialist, which probably means he was a communist when she met him."

"Your mother might've been happier never knowing about her roots."

"Yes, but you don't know my mother. If she finds out now that she's half Russian, she'll immediately find out all the good qualities Russians have and incorporate them for her own. Wait, you'll see—next Christmas she'll probably celebrate it Russian style, or at least the style in which they celebrated it before the country stopped celebrating it at all."

"You're making fun of her."

"No, I'm not. I just know her. She'll hunt down one of those Russian icons in an antique store, and she'll hang it in her loft, and then we'll see her wearing embroidered peasant blouses."

"I don't believe you. You're the romantic in the family; she seems very practical."

"It's not a matter of being romantic versus being pragmatic. It's a matter of living comfortably with this new image of herself. She's got to incorporate that Russian part of herself, or it'll drive her to distraction. Wait, you'll see."

"You never even asked me what *I* am, what kind of a name *Mello* is."

"It doesn't matter."

"That's good, because I have no idea. Mello, it could be anything. Maybe even shortened from something else."

Madelyn wasn't listening, though. At that point she was thinking to herself that Madelyn Mello sounded pretty dumb. Not that changing her name was an issue yet, maybe never would be, although she really didn't believe that. Maddy Mello sounded even worse, but then only her father ever called her Maddy. Mad Mello? It sounded pretty good for a bank robber, not so good for a regular person. And not her initials. Her middle name was Lynn, which would make it M. L. Mello, which was maybe the worst of all.

Eddie was looking at her as though he would like to know what she was thinking. She thought it was a lucky thing for her he couldn't read minds.

THE GOOD THING about her mother's apprehension over meeting her father was that the conversation revolved around that and Eddie was temporarily forgotten. Otherwise, Madelyn knew that her mother would have used this time to question her.

Her mother was looking good, very businesslike in a tweed suit and matching three-quarters' length coat. Her Italian shoes and leather gloves were impeccable, and she was even wearing a felt hat with a feather in its brim, which added a bit of jauntiness to the total look. Madelyn liked the way her mother always managed to look perfect, whatever the occasion, although she wouldn't have been able to manage it herself. Even with her mother's tutelage, she had never got the hang of coordinating outfits. The most she could do was make sure the colors she wore didn't clash.

Shirley was looking a little lost, a little fearful, and this was something new in Madelyn's experience. *She* was usually the one to feel lost or fearful.

"It's not like meeting him is suddenly going to make him your father," Madelyn told her.

"Of course he's my father."

"I don't mean that. Sure, biologically he is, but it's not like you're suddenly going to have him around acting like a father. You'll meet him, and then, if you like him, maybe you'll want to keep in touch. But I'm sure too many years have gone by for either of you to suddenly feel any affection or even necessarily want to be friends." After all, Shirley wasn't even friendly with her mother.

"It's a wonder he's still alive; he must be very old by now."

"Babba said he's five years younger than she."

Shirley started to choke on her sushi and reached for the water glass. Recovering, she said, "That still means he's in his late seventies. My mother always did like younger men."

That was news to Madelyn, but then nothing about Babba would ever surprise her. "Did she have boyfriends while you were growing up?"

"Her friends were always male and always younger, but I don't know whether she actually had boyfriends. If she did, she was discreet about it; I'll say that for her."

Madelyn said, "Babba's crazy about Eddie," then could have bitten her tongue for mentioning him.

"She's always preferred the company of men. Although, to be fair, I don't think women have ever liked her much. She was a little too different for women, but men always seemed to appreciate that difference."

Madelyn started to say something, but her mother wasn't finished.

"I always had lots of girlfriends in school. Oh, I dated, had boyfriends, too, but my close friends were always girls." She paused and looked over at Madelyn. "You were different from both of us, less social. You were always a secretive child, always wanting privacy."

That wasn't at all how Madelyn remembered it. She just remembered feeling left out when her parents were together. If she had been a private sort of child, it had been because she had had no choice.

Shirley said, "I can't say that I entirely approve, but this Eddie of yours has been good for you. And I'm not blind, dear, despite what you may think. I accepted what you told me that day at your apartment, but since then... Well, anyone could see at Christmas that the two of you were in love. I'm glad to see you looking so happy, but I hope you know what you're doing."

Madelyn, who would have liked to have someone's advice, didn't know whether her mother was the right person to ask. Still, there wasn't anyone else. "It's been nice—living with someone, I mean."

"Of course it is, when it's the right person."

"The thing is, today he's over at NYU to see about maybe working there. If he works there he gets free tuition."

"I'm glad to see he wants to make something of himself."

"But things will change. I know they will."

"You'd like to keep him all to yourself, is that it?"

"I don't know; I suppose so."

"Are you afraid he'll meet someone else? Yes, I can tell by your face that's what's bothering you. Life isn't that safe, Madelyn. It's taking chances and risks and hoping for the best. You've got to have some faith in him, and in yourself."

Her mother wasn't telling her anything she hadn't already told herself. It was just that she wasn't used to having faith in herself. She hadn't had the kind of experience that would give her that faith. She did have faith in Eddie, though, so maybe that would suffice.

As THEY APPROACHED the building where Madelyn's grandfather lived, neither of them hurrying, her mother said, "If he's like my mother, I think I'll just turn around and walk out. I don't think I could take two eccentrics in the family."

"Babba probably wasn't like that when they met."

"She was *always* like that. I think she was born that way."

Madelyn had the humorous thought that maybe he would have a stuffed female doll in his apartment, and almost said something about it to her mother, but then she remembered her mother hadn't been to Babba's since she got the doll. And it wasn't something Shirley would find humorous.

She found that some of the anticipation of meeting her grandfather had been dissipated by Eddie's not being with her. She kept wondering what he was doing at NYU and whether he would be discouraged when she saw him later.

Shirley was trying the buzzer on the door when Madelyn saw the window on the second floor open, and then a man with a full head of wavy gray hair stuck his head out the window and called down. "Are you Madelyn?"

"Yes," she shouted up to him.

The next thing that happened was that he threw something out the window at her; she looked at the ground in front of her feet and saw that it was a set of keys.

"Just let youself in," he said. "I'm in 2B."

"That was him?" asked Shirley.

Madelyn nodded, fitting the key into the lock.

"What did he look like?"

"He had a lot of hair, that's all I noticed."

The building didn't appear to be well kept up. The light in the foyer was burned-out, although a dim one on the first landing gave some light on the stairs. There were cigarette butts lying around and the hallway reeked of different smells.

He already had the door open when they got to the second floor. He was tall, so tall he must have dwarfed Babba. He had an interesting face, though, dominated by intelligent eyes and a scimitar of a nose. He was wearing a cardigan over a flannel shirt, and his pants were neatly pressed. On his feet were leather slippers.

"This is my mother, Shirley," Madelyn said to him. "She wanted to meet you, too."

The man gave them a kind smile and asked them inside. "A daughter and a granddaughter all in one day," he said, leading them into the living room.

It was certainly nothing like Babba's apartment. The furniture looked old without looking antique, and the room was neat and clean, without the clutter of Babba's.

"I guess you feel about as strange as I do," he was saying. "How about a cup of coffee? Can I offer you any?"

"Thank you," said Madelyn, just as her mother said, "No, thank you, we just finished eating." Then, looking at Madelyn, Shirley said, "Oh, well, yes a cup of coffee would be nice."

"Ask him about his name," her mother whispered as he went into the kitchen.

Madelyn walked over to the door of the kitchen. He was spooning instant coffee into three cups. He turned when she said, "We were wondering about your name. Mihalenko—what nationality is that?"

He smiled. "You mean you didn't know? Francie never told you?"

Madelyn returned his smile. "The first we even heard of you was three days ago."

"It's Russian. My parents were born in Kiev."

Madelyn couldn't wait to tell Eddie.

"NEVER MIND HIS APARTMENT, what was *he* like?" Eddie asked her. He could tell from the minute she walked in that she was bursting to tell him all about her afternoon, and that was fine with him. He'd rather leave his own story until last.

"He's Russian, Eddie. His parents were actually born there. My great-grandparents. That means Mom's half Russian and I'm a quarter."

"But what was your impression of him? I mean, did you even like him?"

"Oh, he was very nice. Polite, soft-spoken. Just nice, that's all."

"Nice doesn't tell me a thing, Madelyn. Nice is a really meaningless word. I hope you wouldn't describe me to someone as nice."

"But you *are* nice, Eddie."

He groaned and stretched back on the couch. "Did you feel anything for him? Did he feel like your grandfather?"

"No, he felt like a stranger. You know what we mostly talked about? He's been married twice; both of his wives died. But he has five children, not counting Mom, and thirteen grandchildren, and he spent most of the time showing us pictures of them and telling us about them. So I've got all these relatives in New York

I never even knew about, although some of them live out on Long Island.''

"You going to have a big family gathering? Meet everybody?"

"Oh, I doubt that. I don't think I'll even see him again."

"You find some long-lost grandfather and you're not going to even see him again?"

"Eddie, he was polite and all, but he really wasn't interested. He probably hadn't even thought of my mother in fifty years. We didn't mean anything to him, and when I talked to Mom afterward, we realized he didn't really mean anything to us, either. It was about as impersonal as looking up your family tree in the library. He was nice, but there just wasn't any connection."

"What does he do?"

"He's retired. But this is funny, Eddie—he was a subway conductor. You should've seen Mom's face when he said that."

"What's the matter with that? It pays well enough."

"Oh, you'd have to know her to understand. I mean it's better than being a professional anarchist, but still, Mom never takes the subway."

"She'd rather he'd been a cabdriver?"

"No. If she'd had her choice, I'm sure she would have liked him to be a doctor or a judge or something. Mother's very into success."

"I don't think you should be ashamed of any honest job."

"Of course you shouldn't; it's just that some honest jobs have more class than other honest jobs. Take you, for instance. I'm sure she would prefer your having robbed a bank to being a mugger.''

"Bank robbers have more class than muggers?"

"Sure they do."

"You feel that way, too? Like your mom?"

"No, of course not. I didn't care what my grandfather did."

"Yeah, but what about me? What if I'd been a mugger?"

"I don't like muggers," she admitted.

"But you like bank robbers, huh?"

"Eddie, there's a difference."

"Tell me the difference."

"There's something so petty about mugging someone on the street. So personal. And scaring him."

"But it's okay to rob a big, impersonal institution like a bank, is that it? It doesn't matter that you might scare hell out of the tellers?"

"If you don't see any difference, Eddie, why weren't you a mugger?"

"Because you don't get rich being a mugger."

"That's the only reason?"

"Madelyn, I was a kid. I don't know what I might've done. I might've mugged people."

"But you didn't."

"Look, Madelyn, I don't feel like arguing the relative merits of crimes with you. Tell me more about your grandfather."

"That was about it, Eddie. We had coffee, we looked at snapshots, and then we left. Oh, he did tell Mom that not marrying was Babba's idea, although he calls her Francie. He said he wanted to make it legal, but Babba was an advocate of free love in those days."

"You have an interesting family."

"Well, Babba, sure."

"No, all of you. Babba was this free spirit, which her daughter must have rebelled against, becoming in turn very conventional. And then you . . ."

"Yes? What am I?"

"I'm still trying to figure that out."

"So what happened at NYU?"

He tried not to look too pleased about it when he said, "I think I may have a job."

"Really? What kind of a job?"

"Well, I was talking to this woman in personnel, and she had this list of jobs, but most of them were clerical stuff, typists and clerks, things I know nothing about. Then we got to talking about my background, which I was up front about, and she didn't even seem shocked or anything, which was a big relief, and she said that NYU owned all these apartment buildings in the area where faculty live, and the building superintendent in one of the buildings was quitting, and would I be interested?"

"A super? You'd be a *super*?"

"Listen, Madelyn, I'm not qualified for much. You don't exactly get on-the-job training in prison, you know. I didn't figure I was even qualified for this, but she said I didn't have to do electrical or plumbing—for stuff like that I'd just call in an expert. It's mostly taking out the trash and keeping the halls clean and taking complaints."

"Oh, Eddie, that seems so demeaning."

"I'm telling you, Madelyn, you have some strange ideas about what's demeaning. Being in prison is demeaning. As far as that goes—and I don't want you taking this wrong—living off you is demeaning." Then he saw the way her face began to crumple and he said, "Not *with* you, Madelyn. Living with you is about as far as you can get from demeaning. I'm talking about letting you support me. I'm tired of being taken care of. I want to start taking care of myself."

"I'm sorry, I shouldn't have said that—about it being demeaning."

"And I don't want you being sorry for saying what you think, either. I figure we should be able to say whatever we think to each other and not have to worry about the consequences."

"So you're going to take the job?"

"If they offer it, I'm taking it. Madelyn, I don't think you understand how perfect it is. I'll be an employee of NYU, so I'll get my tuition paid, plus have plenty of time to study. And what's best—listen to this—I get a free apartment, utilities paid. Also a salary, but it's pretty small. Still, all I'm going to need is money for food, maybe textbooks. It solves all my problems. It's perfect. I can't even believe how perfect it is."

"You're moving out?"

"Hey, don't look like that. This was supposed to be temporary, until I found my own place."

"But now we love each other."

"That's not going to change, Madelyn. Nothing I've been telling you is going to change that."

But already he could sense a change in her.

Chapter Ten

After that, suddenly nothing seemed right. Just that one visit to NYU and Eddie appeared changed. For one thing, he wanted to get out of the apartment all the time. It was as though he couldn't wait to move, couldn't stand to be alone with her anymore.

Well, maybe that was an exaggeration. They still made love and that was good. It was still good to wake up next to him in the morning. But now it felt temporary, which in fact it was. And since she knew it was, it colored everything they did together. The world, which just yesterday had seemed perfect to her, now was showing fault lines she hadn't anticipated.

She made a real effort to go along with what he wanted. He said to her, "Madelyn, show me the city. I don't even know my own way around yet."

And so she showed him her favorite parts of the city. She took him to Lincoln Center one morning, where for only a couple of dollars they were able to sit in on the rehearsal of the Philharmonic. One day they went to the Metropolitan Museum of Art and later had tea in the Palm Court of the Plaza Hotel. They went to see a Russian film that her mother, now into her Russian phase, was touting, but they both were bored by it. She tried to explain the subway system to him, but she didn't know it very well herself. The cold spell had broken and she liked going places with Eddie, but they seemed to be losing their closeness.

She even gave in to him about New Year's Eve. She would have preferred staying home, out of the crowds, but he had his heart set on going to Times Square to see the new year in, and that's where they went.

They walked up there around ten o'clock, and the weather was good, not too cold. A couple of blocks from Forty-second Street and Broadway, the crowd began to thicken and she held on tightly to his hand, wanting more than anything to turn around and head back home.

"I've never seen so many people in one place," Eddie said. "Have you?"

They had been walking at a fast pace but now they were practically standing still, moving only inches in the same amount of time they had been moving yards. "A few times," she told him, thinking of the World Series game her father had taken her to once and a St. Patrick's Day crowd she had been caught in a couple of years ago.

They passed a subway entrance and she felt an overwhelming urge to run down the stairs and get a train back to the Village. She hated crowds, hated the feeling of being trapped, of having to go along with the crowd's movements, her freedom of choice taken away from her. She thought of saying something to Eddie, asking him if he had changed his mind, but when she looked at him she saw he was enjoying it. She tried to convince herself that she wasn't in a crowd, that she was alone with Eddie and that other people just happened to be around.

"This is amazing," Eddie kept saying as they approached Times Square. "I've seen it on television, but it's different when you're a part of it."

The crowd was mixture of tourists and New Yorkers and Time Square regulars, the latter noisy and drunk and very likely containing a few thieves. She kept her hand on her shoulder bag, hugging it to her body, although they were so tightly pressed in by the people at that point it seemed unnecessary. A man on her right was breathing whiskey fumes into her face, making her feel nauseated.

Midnight was still half an hour away when she saw Eddie's face break out in a sweat and he appeared to turn pale, although it could have been the neon lights. "You okay?" she asked him.

"I feel like I'm locked in."

"We *are* locked in."

He began looking around, as though for an escape, and she sensed the beginnings of panic in his movements. "You want to try to get out of here, Eddie?"

"I'm sorry I got you into this."

"Don't worry about that."

"The thing is, I don't think we could get out of here if we wanted to."

"We can try."

"Look, Madelyn, if you want to stick around for midnight, I'm okay."

But he didn't look okay; he was beginning to look terrible. "Come on, Eddie," she said, turning against the crowd and trying to pull him between the people wedged tightly in front of them. "Excuse me," she kept saying, getting disgruntled looks and bleary smiles. It seemed like an impossibility, but she kept making her way slowly through the crowd for what seemed like hours, but finally they were through the bulk of it and on the outskirts, where there was at least breathing space.

"Is this better?" she asked him. "We can probably still see from here."

He was pushing back his sweaty hair with one hand and taking deep breaths. "I guess this wasn't one of my greatest ideas."

She didn't want to say anything that sounded like "I told you so." Instead, she said, "Why don't we get a drink? I think we're the only ones not drunk yet."

"Sounds good, but why don't we head back to your neighborhood first. That way we won't have too far to walk home if we get loaded."

They ended up—past midnight—in the neighborhood bar he had taken a liking to, which was also crowded, but manageably so.

And then there was just New Year's Day left, because the woman from NYU had called and the job was Eddie's if he could move in on January 2. Eddie had said he could.

She couldn't help waking up depressed on the first day of January. And in addition to being depressed, she also thought she might have a hangover. They had had more to drink on New Year's Eve than usual and now her head was testimony to the fact that drinking didn't really agree with her.

When he said good morning and kissed her, when she fixed them breakfast, when they ate together and when Eddie cleaned up, each and every thing had the feeling of being the last time, and it wasn't right. It had been so perfect between them and she didn't see why it had to end.

A job, sure. She knew he had to get a job. But she hadn't anticipated the job coming with an apartment. She had been sure that it would be a long time before he was able to afford to move into an apartment, and by then she didn't think he would want to. The only hope she had was that she knew what a super's apartment would be like. It would be some small, dark place, probably in the basement, and maybe Eddie would realize once he moved in that he couldn't stand it. It would probably remind him of his prison cell. She would say, "Oh, Eddie, you can't live like this," and he would agree, and then they'd go back home together. Maybe it was wishful thinking, but it was the only kind of thinking she felt like doing.

"How about a game of Scrabble?" Eddie asked her after the dishes were done.

"I don't feel like it."

"You don't feel like Scrabble? I thought you always felt like Scrabble."

She knew he was trying to make her smile, but she didn't feel like smiling, either.

"I guess we could watch the bowl games."

"Go ahead if you like."

"I had ten years of bowl games. I'm sick of bowl games."

She went over to the couch and sat down on what was now "her" end. "Can we talk, Eddie?"

"Of course we can talk." But he wasn't joining her on the couch, he was still standing there, leaning against the kitchen counter.

"I know you had to get a job, Eddie. I understand that."

"And I know you're upset about my moving out."

"I can't help it."

"Tell me something, Madelyn. When you moved out of your parents' place into this apartment, how did you feel?"

"I don't know; I don't remember."

"Try. I'd really like to know."

"It made me feel grown-up. I thought my whole life would change when I moved in here."

"Did it?"

"No." She wanted to say that her whole life had changed since he had moved in, but she lacked the courage.

"Listen to me, Madelyn. I have never in my life lived alone. I have never just lived like a normal person. I have never bought a piece of furniture or a picture for my wall or even had a pet or a plant like those you have, something to take care of. I've never even been out on a date."

"*That's* what you want to do? *Date?*"

"You're not listening to me. If by that you mean do I want to go out with other women, the answer is no. But I'd like to date you. I'd like to be able to call you on the phone and ask you out to the movies, then pick you up and take you home afterward. I missed out on all that, Madelyn.''

''You want to go from living together to dating?''

He finally crossed over to the couch, but he didn't sit close to her. ''When you say it like that it sounds stupid, but it really isn't. I'd just like to go back and start over with you like a normal person. I've loved it here, and I can't believe you don't know that. But I need this, Madelyn.''

''It'll never be the same.''

''Look, I know what you're thinking. You're afraid I'm going to walk out of here and everything is going to change. Well, some things will change, but that doesn't mean it'll be for the worse. My love for you isn't going to change, Madelyn. I don't know about you, but I figure we'll end up married. But that's not going to be until I can earn my own way, and that's going to take a while. It might not bother you to live off your parents, but it sure as hell bothers me.''

''You really think we'll get married?'' That was the only part of Eddie's speech she wanted to hear.

''If it's up to me we will.''

''Meaning if I don't ruin everything.''

''Madelyn, if you told me right now that if I leave you'll never see me again, it'd break my heart, but I'd still go. I want to be able to live with you, but I've got to be able to live with myself, too. And I couldn't live with myself if I stayed here much longer.''

''Does this mean we won't make love any-more?''

"Come on, I'm going to be a super, not a monk. We've got all our lives left, we don't have to rush things."

She hated herself for what she was doing. She would have loved to be cool and just agree with him, but she didn't feel cool. She felt terrible. And because she felt terrible, she wanted him to feel terrible. And she didn't like herself for that.

What she really wanted, what she was hoping he would do, was to ask her to move in with him. She would have, she would have gone anywhere with him, but he wasn't even asking. She could understand his need to live alone for the first time. It was just that she was tired of living alone. She felt as if she had always lived alone. She could only hope that he wouldn't like it, that he would miss her so much he'd call her up after a couple of days and beg her to move in with him.

Except she knew him well enough by now to know that wasn't likely to happen.

EDDIE WAS TRYING as hard as he could to sound as sad about leaving as she was feeling, but he knew he wasn't managing very well. To tell the truth, he was feeling the same sort of anticipation he had felt right before he was released from prison. He knew nothing between them was really going to change. He was never going to love someone else the way he loved her. He knew she was feeling insecure, feeling she was being left alone, but he didn't consider it leaving her at all. On the contrary, he had gone to NYU first, rather than one of the other schools, in the hope that he'd still be near her.

He finally talked her into a game of Scrabble. He didn't say, "Let's play a final game of Scrabble," but she was acting as if that's what it was. Just from the words she formed he could tell the state of her mind. "Depress," that was one she used. And "alone." So he was surprised when she said, "Would you mind if I went over to see how Babba's doing?"

"Of course not. Let's go," he said, thinking that getting out of the apartment for a while might help things.

"I meant alone."

That was a shocker. He couldn't remember the last time she had wanted to do anything alone. In fact, he could never remember a time. "Sure, go on. I'll just watch a little football while you're gone."

He stayed on the couch as she bundled up, hoping she would talk to Babba about his moving out. He was sure that Babba would agree with him, think it was the right thing to do. Although one thing he had learned, you could never determine in advance what Babba was going to think about anything.

After she left, he turned on the TV, but he found he couldn't concentrate on the game. He had never played football as a kid—in fact, he had never played any team sports—so he didn't find it very interesting. He had done a little boxing in the joint; just about everyone did a little boxing in prison. It let off steam and was one of the few activities provided. Anyway, most of the guys had been pretty good fighters before they even got there.

He'd been in his share of fights as a kid, probably more than his share. He hadn't been all that big, for one thing, so he had to show he was tough since he didn't look it. He hadn't even attained his full height until he was in prison. He didn't feel like fighting anymore, but it still gave him a good feeling to know he could defend himself on the streets if it was ever necessary. And in the city it might be.

Thinking about prison made him think about Madelyn's letters, or rather, his letters to Madelyn. He thought he'd read some of them over again, ones he hadn't read before. Then he thought he'd suggest to her that maybe they get rid of all the letters, maybe make a ceremony of burning them. Start anew.

Except that was maybe the dumbest idea he'd ever had. It would probably be the determining factor in convincing her that he really was walking out for good. No, he sure as hell wouldn't mention that.

He went over to the cupboard and reached in for the file folder in the back, one he hadn't looked at before, then got himself a beer before taking them both back to the couch.

He probably wouldn't have paid any attention to the newspaper clippings inside the folder if one hadn't fallen out right in front of his eyes. He saw it was about a bank robbery, wondered what it was doing in there, then wondered if maybe she had gone to the library and got an old copy of a New Jersey paper that had a write-up on him.

Only it wasn't about his bank job; it was another one entirely. He read it over, couldn't see why it had interested her, then dumped the whole file out and saw the clippings piling up.

What the hell was Madelyn doing keeping accounts of all those bank robberies? He read some of them, didn't find them particularly interesting, then put them back in the file along with his letters, which he had lost interest in reading.

He had known she had romanticized his own bank job, romanticized him to an extent as a bank robber, but this was ridiculous. Was that what she wanted him to do? Was she secretly hoping he'd revert to his former ways just to liven up her life?

That didn't sound like the Madelyn he knew. Yet, maybe he really didn't know her. She had corresponded with a convict, after all. Right now, if she told him she was going to correspond with another convict, well, he wouldn't think that was such a great idea. In fact, he wouldn't like it at all. He would even find it a little strange. For one thing, now that he knew her, it didn't seem in character. She just wasn't the type to write to a criminal.

She wanted him to rob a bank. He couldn't find any other reason for her to cut out all those damn articles about bank robberies. Maybe she wanted to do it with him. Maybe she thought it would be some kind of thrill. Well, maybe she was right. It had been thrilling, at least he had thought so at nineteen. It was for damn sure prison hadn't been thrilling, though. And it would be just like her to romanticize prison, too. Maybe she thought it was fun and games.

What he found romantic these days was getting a job and going to school. And his own place. He would have loved to talk to her about that, but he sensed it wasn't something she wanted to hear about.

Bank robberies. He couldn't believe it. Hell, maybe she was more like Babba than he had thought. The only thing he could figure was that he was likely the only criminal she had ever known, and because she loved him she was prepared to love a life of crime, was prepared to join him in it.

He couldn't believe it. If she was hiding that from him, what else was she hiding? She needed to be taught a lesson, that was for sure. But if teaching her a lesson meant robbing a bank, count him out. He had learned his lesson and didn't need another one.

Now that he knew about it, though, he had to do something. Teach her a lesson without actually robbing a bank. Call her bluff.

At least he was better at calling bluffs than he was at robbing banks.

MADELYN WAS EVEN MORE DEJECTED when she left Babba than when she had arrived. First off, when Madelyn told Babba about Eddie's job and apartment, all Babba said was "That's good." Then she wanted to hear about the reunion between Shirley and her father.

After that, after she had finished telling Babba every detail, and when she started to tell Babba how she was feeling about Eddie's moving out, Babba changed the subject again and started in on Albania. *Albania!* Madelyn didn't even know where Albania was.

When she finally finished with Albania and Madelyn tried once more to shift the conversation to Eddie, Babba said, "You're just like your mother." It didn't sound like a compliment.

"I'm not at all like Mother," Madelyn protested.

"Only interested in yourself, your own problems. You're not starving in Africa. You're not living on one square foot of sidewalk in India. Your country isn't disappearing under rubble like Lebanon. Quit feeling sorry for yourself, Madelyn. I can't stand crybabies."

Madelyn figured she could've got more sympathy from a stranger in the streets.

In a way, though, she had been wrong to go to Babba with her problems. It was Eddie she should be talking to. But even then, talking wasn't going to change anything. She could tell Eddie had his mind made up, and she either had to go along with him or forget about him. And she knew she couldn't forget about him. So she was just going to have to go along with him and hope the move didn't damage or destroy their relationship.

Eddie seemed pretty cheerful when she got home. The only place she had found open was McDonald's, so she brought back hamburgers and fries for them. This cheered Eddie up even more.

They were sitting at the table eating and not saying much, although Madelyn could sense he had something to say. He kept looking at her, and sometimes he was smiling when he looked at her, and finally it got to her and she said, "Okay, what is it?"

"What is what?" he said, trying to look innocent.

"I know there's something on your mind."

"How'd you know?"

"Come on, let's not play guessing games."

But Eddie didn't say anything until he had finished off his second Big Mac and downed his beer; then he went to the refrigerator and opened another one. He asked her if she wanted one, but she didn't. She wanted to hear what he had to say.

"I had this idea, Madelyn," he said, and his eyes had an excited look to them.

He's going to ask me to move in with him, she was thinking, and she knew her own eyes were beginning to look excited. "What is it?" she asked, trying to keep the excitement out of her voice.

"I think I've figured out a way we can be together."

She didn't know why it had taken him so long. She had figured it out days ago. "Tell me."

"I don't have to be a super, you know."

You can be a super and I'll move in with you, she wanted to say, but she kept silent. He seemed to be waiting for her to say something, so she said, "What're you getting at, Eddie?"

"Now don't hit the ceiling, Madelyn."

"I'm going to hit you if you don't get to the point pretty quick."

"I was thinking we could rob a bank."

Her Big Mac felt as if it were going to come back up. She tried to stay calm, or at least appear calm, but it was just about the last thing she'd expected to hear. She couldn't believe Eddie was even saying it. Had she been living with someone she didn't even know all this time? She began to feel a little frightened, and the fact that she was, frightened her still more.

"You know that bank over on Sixth Avenue?"

Sure she knew it. She had fantasized robbing it about a dozen times. She nodded.

"It'd be easy, Madelyn—a piece of cake. In, out and down into the subway before anyone even noticed."

"Are you serious about this, Eddie?" Still hardly believing it. Eddie? Who had said he had done it when he was a stupid kid? Who had said he wasn't *that* stupid anymore?

He spread his arms, looking proud of himself. "It would solve everything," he explained, drawing out the "everything," making it sound as if he were handing her a Christmas present.

And then, like one of those cartoon characters over whose head a light bulb appears, she knew. She just knew that Eddie had been in her files and had found the clippings. In her private files, where he had no business to be. Only that wasn't quite fair. She had told him his letters were in there, and she certainly wouldn't have objected to his reading his own letters.

He was watching her, waiting for a reaction. Testing her. Trying to find out why she had cut out those articles. Probably sure that her reaction would be shock and dismay, and then he would lecture her on being so interested in bank robberies. The fright had turned to a slow-burning anger, and she decided to turn the tables on him.

She gave him a serious look, then slowly began to smile. "You're right, it *would* solve everything."

He didn't say anything, but now he was watching her as though she were a bomb about to explode.

"And you could do it *right* this time, Eddie; you're not a stupid kid anymore. And I could help you."

He appeared to be incapable of speech.

"That was a good choice, Eddie. That bank, I mean. Once you're out the door you're practically in the subway entrance. And the Sixth Avenue as well as the Eighth Avenue subways are there. If we timed it right, like during rush hour on Friday when the bank stays open late, we would be out and into the crowd so fast they'd never catch us. And the banks must be filled with money on Friday, all the people cashing their paychecks."

He finally spoke. "It sounds as though you've given this some thought."

She shrugged. "I'm just throwing ideas around. What about you? You have any ideas?"

"I hadn't really made a plan yet."

"Disguises, too," she said, trying to act more excited by the minute. "We could have reversible coats, and the bank would give out a description of two people in red coats, only as soon as we got inside the subway station, we could take them off and turn them inside out, and *voilá*, blue coats. And since it's winter, it wouldn't look strange to have mufflers around our faces or our hats pulled down low."

"I don't believe this." He sounded totally disoriented.

"You don't believe what? You don't like my ideas?"

"I don't believe you're going along with it."

"You didn't think I'd have the guts?"

He was shaking his head. "You think it's all right just to go out and rob a bank? You think it's some kind of *game*?"

She shrugged. "Something like that. It'd be a lot more fun than Scrabble."

"I figured you were so honest."

"Well, it's not like a mugging, Eddie. I mean it's only a bank. Who cares about banks?"

"But someone could get hurt."

"Not if they do what we say."

"What are you, some kind of convict groupie?"

"Is that what you think?"

He was looking thoroughly confused. "I don't know what I think."

"Does that mean the bank robbery's off?"

"I didn't think you'd be like this."

"Like what?"

"Like a . . . like a common criminal."

She paused a moment before saying, in a deadly tone, "And I didn't think you'd look in my private files."

His mouth dropped open, then he sagged in his chair and began to smile. Then he was laughing.

She just sat there staring at him, not joining in the merriment.

"You knew all the time," he said, once he got his laughter under control.

"No, not all the time. At first I thought you were serious. But it just didn't sound like you."

"You think it sounded like *you*?"

"You believed me, though, didn't you? You really thought I was going to rob a bank with you."

"Don't try to sound so innocent, Madelyn. Why did you save all those clippings about bank jobs?"

"Not in order to rob a bank."

"Why else?"

She thought of all her fantasies, but she knew he wouldn't understand. *She* hardly understood them. "I don't know. I guess you just got me interested in it."

"Why? Why, of all the things about me, did you choose that?"

"I'm not the only one, Eddie. Everyone thinks it's interesting. I guess it's the kind of thing a lot of people fantasize about but don't have the guts to do."

"You *fantasize* about it?"

That had been the wrong analogy to give him. "I thought about it. Remember that movie we watched, *Dog Day Afternoon*?"

He nodded, still not looking appeased.

"Well, it was hard not to think about how I would've done it differently."

"But if I had been really serious, Madelyn, would you have gone out and robbed a bank with me?"

"Of course not. For the few moments I thought you were serious I was appalled."

Now, in a perverse way, he looked disappointed. "You mean you don't love me enough to do it? What would you have done if I had been serious, turned me in?"

"This isn't fair, Eddie. But I'll tell you, if you *had* been serious, then you wouldn't have been the man I fell in love with. If you had shown up that first day with plans to continue your criminal career, you wouldn't be here now."

He sighed. "That's a relief."

"Although I might have been attracted to you."

"That's allowed."

She got up and went over to his side of the table, putting her arms around his neck and resting her chin on his head. "But it *would* solve everything."

"Sure it would; we'd both be in prison."

"Didn't you think my ideas were good?"

"A lot better than River Rat's."

"I don't like that bank anyway."

"Madelyn!"

"Eddie, I'm only joking." But she wasn't. She really didn't like that bank.

Chapter Eleven

The former super was going to be there to "show him the ropes," the woman at the placement office had told Eddie, and when he got there about noon on January 2, he was buzzed in and then met at the door by a guy a few years younger than Eddie, short and muscular, with a full head of black hair and a mustache that reached to the collar of his shirt.

"You Eddie?" he was asked, and when Eddie nodded, the young man held out his hand to him and said, "Trumbull Atkins, but you can call me Bull."

Eddie shook his hand, trying not to grin at the name, but then Bull said, "Hey, it's okay to laugh; everyone does," and Eddie chuckled.

"I got my stuff moved out already; moving in with my lady. It's a good deal here, though; the apartment's not bad and the free tuition and all. I assume you'll be going to NYU."

Eddie nodded again and started to say something, but Bull didn't give him the chance. "The building's in pretty good shape, so you don't get many complaints, although watch out for Professor McGinley, he's always reporting prowlers in the hall. What they are, usually, are guests of one of the other profs, but McGinley, since he never entertains, doesn't understand that other people do.''

By now Bull had led him back to one of the first-floor apartments, and Eddie was really surprised when he got a look at the place. The living room was as big as Madelyn's entire apartment, and there was also a separate kitchen, although it wasn't big enough for a table, and a fair-sized bedroom. It was partially furnished, enough for his needs, and Bull told him the furniture came with the place.

''Why would you want to give this up?'' Eddie asked him.

''Now that I'm graduating, I'll be getting a job, and you can't be a super and work full time, too. I was thinking maybe graduate school, but my old lady accused me of using it as an excuse not to move in with her, so I finally capitulated.''

''What exactly do I have to do?''

''The biggest thing is the boiler. I got it aced, though, can teach you in a couple of hours. You ever worked with a boiler?''

''No. I've never even seen one.''

''No problem; I hadn't, either. Other than that, and making sure the heat's working, it's just little stuff like taking out the trash barrels and keeping the entry hall clean and shoveling the snow on the walk and such. That might sound like a lot coming all at once, but it isn't. You don't even have to be around to take the complaints. I have a telephone answering machine I used, but mostly they'll just put notes under your door if the tenants don't find you in. Then you call a plumber or an electrician or whatever they need and get it billed to NYU.''

"Did you go to school full-time days?" Eddie asked him, wondering how he should schedule his classes.

"No. Mostly I went late afternoons and evenings. For a couple of reasons. One, evening is when most of the complaints came in, so I liked to be out. And two, cleaning the sidewalk's got to be done in the morning. Also, I like to sleep late. That way I didn't have to take Lisa out during the week, just on weekends. But do it whatever way you want.''

"I'm not even sure I'll get accepted at NYU."

"You work for them, they'll get you in. I can tell just by looking at you you're not right out of high school. You a transfer?"

"What's that?"

"You know, like are you transferring from another school?"

"I took correspondence courses.''

"Oh, yeah? I couldn't do that, not on my own. I don't have that kind of discipline. Also, I like the social life.''

"I was in prison," said Eddie, not thinking much about it.

Bull did a double take. "That for real?"

"Last ten years."

Bull was looking clearly agitated, which surprised Eddie. The woman in personnel had seemed to find it interesting, as had all the women who knew. But Bull, who he would have thought would just shrug it off, was suddenly looking nervous.

"I robbed a bank," he told him, thinking that this would calm him down.

But "I wouldn't tell any of the tenants if I were you" was what he said.

Eddie supposed it was a good thing not everyone viewed bank robbers in a romantic light, but now he wished he had kept his mouth shut.

"Hey, I know you've done your time and everything, I was just a little surprised is all. I'm sure the city is filled with ex-cons, but I've never known any at NYU. They usually don't go in for academia, if you know what I mean."

Eddie didn't even know what "academia" meant. "I was just a stupid kid," he said, wondering why he felt he had to make excuses to Bull.

"Yeah, weren't we all." But obviously Bull hadn't been that stupid.

Bull took him down into the basement and explained the workings of the boiler to him, then said, "Listen, any problems, just give me a call. I'll leave you my number. I can even come over and help you out if it's a real emergency."

Then, back at the apartment, Bull said, "Listen, want to get a drink somewhere? I'll show you the neighborhood. I figure I got about three hours of freedom left, might as well do something with it."

Eddie had planned on getting settled in, then phoning Madelyn and seeing if she wanted to go out to dinner, but Bull was being so helpful he didn't want to refuse. Anyway, he could still do that later.

Eddie found out Bull was very, very good at something, and that something was drinking. He was trying to match him beer for beer at one of the local college hangouts, but by the time Bull took off for his lady's place, Eddie couldn't do any more than just find his apartment and make it to the bed. It didn't have sheets or a blanket or even a pillow, but he was out in a matter of seconds and didn't wake up until the next morning.

EDDIE WOKE UP disoriented. Not only didn't he know where he was at first, but he felt as if he'd rather be dead. Gradually it came back to him, the pitcher after pitcher of beer he and Bull had consumed. What he couldn't remember was how he got home. For this was home, he now knew.

He sat up on the side of the bed, his head pleading with him not to make any fast moves. There were about a million things he needed, and at the top of that list was aspirin, but he didn't even have that. Or coffee. Or even a cup if he had coffee. Or even a pot to boil water in.

Sheets, a blanket, towels—oh, hell, the list was endless. And he didn't dare spend the last of his money on any of it. Nor did he know when he got paid. Not that it was much, but it would cover the essentials. Forget taking Madelyn out to dinner, though; he didn't have the money to feed himself.

In his elation at getting the job and free tuition and a free apartment, it hadn't occurred to him that maybe he couldn't live on two hundred dollars a month, especially after deductions. As for his ideas for fixing up his own place, he was damn lucky it came with the furnishings it did or he'd be sleeping on the floor.

He was just going to have to find some way to make some extra income. Bull had told him they had a contractor that painted the apartments, but maybe he could do that himself.

He got out the wallet he had bought—thankfully he had got a cheap one—and counted his money. Eighty-seven dollars and change. Okay, there were certain necessities he had to have. Like one towel, a bar of soap, maybe an old army blanket from the surplus store. A saucepan for water and some instant coffee. A cup. Some cans of soup. A bowl and a spoon and a can opener. A loaf of bread and some bologna, so he didn't starve to death.

And my, wasn't he feeling sorry for himself. There had been a time when just having his freedom would have been enough, now he was grousing because he couldn't afford McDonald's. He'd make out. There were always honest ways to make a little extra money if a person was willing to work. And he was willing. He'd get to know the tenants and maybe be able to do some odd jobs for them. He could always clean apartments and was pretty handy with a hammer if anyone needed shelves put in.

He had become spoiled at Madelyn's. He was free, wasn't he? Everything else was secondary.

Except aspirin. Right now aspirin wasn't secondary at all.

After he'd picked up the things he needed and stowed them away in the apartment, he went over to the admissions office and filled out all the forms necessary for admission. When he went in for an interview he got a couple of shocks. The high school equivalency he had earned in prison was okay, but he was told that the correspondence courses he had spent so much money on would not be accepted for credit.

"I'm sorry," the counsellor told him, "but the school isn't accredited. One thing, though, it'll help you in your accounting courses."

Eddie had thought he would have had at least two years of school under his belt, but instead he had to start as a freshman. Probably the oldest freshman in the school.

"I see you're working for the school," Mr. Samuels said.

Eddie nodded.

"The job shouldn't be that demanding. If you take a full schedule and go year round, you ought to be able to get your degree in three years."

Eddie felt stupid complaining about three years when he had already wasted ten with nothing to show for it.

Mr. Samuels was saying, "There might be schools who would give you credit for those courses."

"Would they be any good?"

"Probably not."

He was given a catalog and schedule of courses and told when to come back for registration. What bothered him most of all wasn't the three years ahead of him, it was the three years before he would have anything to offer to Madelyn. Maybe it wasn't worth trying to get a degree. Maybe he should try to get into some trade where he could make some money right away.

In her apartment she had made him feel like an equal, but he was far from that. He had more than he should have expected to have, but not nearly enough to meet Madelyn's expectations. Or her family's. And he couldn't blame them. Why should she waste her time on some poor college student, anyway?

A little more self-pity, huh, Eddie boy? he asked himself. It was just that it was so damn strange being on his own. No one to talk to. No one to share things with. More self-pity. He'd only been on his own one day, for God's sake. Wasn't he a survivor? Wasn't that what he had always told himself?

And, after all, no one had ever told him living honestly was going to be easy.

MADELYN DIDN'T STIR from her apartment the day Eddie moved out.

He had told her he was meeting the guy he was taking over for, so she didn't ask to go along. She counted off the minutes: how much time it would take him to walk over to Washington Square, how long to learn the rudiments of the job, a few minutes to unpack his belongings, a few more minutes in case she hadn't given him enough time.

She couldn't concentrate on anything. Not on reading, not on watching television, not even on the game of solitaire she dealt out. She was just waiting, waiting for the phone to ring.

She experienced an odd sort of déjà vu when the buzzer sounded. She immediately thought it was Eddie, but it turned out to be the mail carrier with the oversized book she had expected the day Eddie had arrived. Disappointed, she took it from the man, then closed and locked the door. She used a knife to open the box it came in.

She barely glanced at the book. She wasn't interested in exercise or pictures of Jane Fonda or in reading or in anything else that didn't include Eddie.

When dinner hour came and passed with still no call from him, she fixed herself a frozen dinner, even then taking her time to eat it in case he called and suggested they go out to eat.

It was easily the longest day of her life. It was hard to accept his never even calling after their having been inseparable for the past few weeks. Was he able just to walk out and forget her? Was something like that even possible?

Shortly before midnight, she carried his files of letters up into her loft bed and began to read them from the beginning. Surprisingly, they were boring. They weren't at all like the Eddie she had come to love. They were coolly impersonal, when she wanted intimacy.

She didn't fantasize about robbing a bank that night. Instead, she fantasized about Eddie's moving back in with her, telling her he had been wrong and he'd never leave her again.

The trouble was, the bank robbing fantasies had seemed more real.

"Suzanna? It's Madelyn."

"Oh, hi, Mad, how're things going?"

"Well—"

"That was some Christmas, wasn't it? I was telling my folks about it and they were sorry to miss it. Listen, did you ever meet that grandfather of yours?"

"I was wondering, Suzanna, if we could meet for lunch."

"I'd love to, but I don't have a baby-sitter and it's no pleasure schlepping a toddler to a restaurant. Listen, why don't you come over here? I don't have much, but I could fix you a grilled-cheese sandwich."

"You're sure you don't mind?"

"Mind? It'll be great to have an adult to talk to for a change."

"Thanks, Suzanna. I'll be there in about an hour."

It was too painful sitting and waiting for the phone to ring. Picking up the receiver every so often to see if the phone was really in order. Afraid to leave the house for fear it would ring when she was gone. He could have called her by now. If he cared, he would have.

Anyway, she needed someone to talk to. She had never confided in Suzanna before, but she had sensed at Christmas that Suzanna was someone she could talk to. And even if she were wrong, it would serve to get her out of the house. If Eddie called he could just wonder where she was, rather than her having to wonder about him.

She had never been to Suzanna's apartment, even though her cousin had been married for five years. Not that she had ever been invited, but she could have called up before this and suggested lunch.

She took a taxi to the East Side and found that Suzanna lived in a fairly new, modern building between

First and Second Avenue. There was no doorman, but there was an impressive security system complete with a concierge in the lobby. The man had to call up to Suzanna to verify that Madelyn was expected before she was allowed to use the elevator.

When Suzanna answered the door she was wearing the kind of outfit Jane Fonda had had on in the exercise book, even to the leg warmers crumpled down around her ankles.

"The kid's asleep, so we won't be disturbed for a while," she told Madelyn, although Madelyn would have liked seeing Brian.

Suzanna took her coat and hung it up, then said, "Let's hear the scoop about the long-lost relative."

Madelyn gave her an abbreviated version while the sandwiches were cooking, then, when they sat down to eat, she said, "I need your advice, Suzanna."

"You're pregnant, right?"

Madelyn felt herself flush. "No, of course not. Why would you say a thing like that?"

Suzanna shrugged. "I just couldn't think of anything else I could give you advice on."

"No, it's about Eddie." She went on to explain about his job and his moving out.

"Hey, that was luck, wasn't it? I bet he never dreamed he'd walk out of prison and into something like that. Not bad, and those NYU buildings are prime real estate."

"I just didn't think he'd move out."

"You working, Mad?"

She shook her head.

"Your parents still supporting you?"

"I suppose so."

"Men have some pride, you know, and the ones who don't aren't worth getting mixed up with."

"I miss him."

"Sure you do, but you'll still see him. Just figure you two were on a vacation, and now it's back to the real world."

"I'm tired of being alone. I've done all the things I want to do alone. Does that make any sense to you?"

"Oh, sure. On the other hand, I could use a little of that aloneness these days. I'm never alone. I can't even close the bathroom door anymore."

Madelyn could tell she was sounding like a spoiled, sorry-for-herself brat. "You didn't find a nursery school?"

"They all have waiting lists. Practically all the mothers work these days, at least in Manhattan, and the ones who don't generally only have one kid and want that kid to have some companionship. I think I should have had another right away so Brain would have had someone to play with."

"I tried to find a job in a nursery school once."

"Yeah? What would you want to do that for?"

"I like children."

"So what happened?"

"They weren't interested because my degree's in business."

"So open your own. A degree in business for a business owner wouldn't be half bad."

"I couldn't do that."

"Why not? Don't you ever want to work, Mad? I mean, granted, I could use a little free time myself, but doesn't it get boring when that's all you have?"

"Most of the jobs I've tried have been just as boring. Plus, I wasn't any good at them."

"But if you like children, maybe you wouldn't be bored. And I'll tell you something, Mad, if you don't mind some advice."

"No, I'd appreciate it."

"With Eddie in school full time, you're going to need something to do or you'll be climbing the walls. You'll be sitting at home worrying about all those coeds he'll be meeting."

She hadn't even thought of that. Eddie would be meeting all sorts of interesting women going to school, and all she'd be doing would be staying home and stagnating. "I wouldn't even know how to go about it."

"What's the problem? You find a space and advertise. You got one kid in advance."

"I'd have to think about it."

"Of course you would. No one jumps into something like that without a little planning."

"Would I need a license or anything?"

"Probably. But I don't see why you couldn't get one. You're going to need capital, too, but you might be able to swing a bank loan. Your folks would co-sign for you, wouldn't they?"

"I suppose."

"Or you could get Eddie to rob a bank for you."

Madelyn saw that she was joking, and she couldn't help smiling herself, and that reminded her of what Eddie had done and she told her cousin about it.

Suzanna was laughing out loud by the time she was halfway into the story. "But why were you keeping those clippings?"

"I'll tell you something worse that even Eddie doesn't know about. I've been planning all these bank robberies in my mind. He'd kill me if he knew."

"I'd do the same thing. As soon as I found out at Christmas where he'd been, I thought, finally we have someone interesting in the family. Not that he's exactly in the family, but you know what I mean."

"Babba's interesting."

"Yeah, but she's not related to me. That was only the second time I've ever seen her."

"I've really enjoyed this, Suzanna. I feel a whole lot better now than when I came over here."

"You going to do it, then?"

"I didn't say that."

"I'll tell you what, Mad, if you decide to set up a nursery school, I'll go in with you."

"Go in with me?"

"Why not? I have to stay home all day with one kid anyway. I might as well take care of more kids and make some money doing it."

"You like kids?"

"Of course I like kids; I have one, don't I? And listen, I'm fluent in French. We can teach all those little kids French."

"You think they'll like that?"

Suzanna grinned. "No, but their mothers sure as hell will. We could pick out some French name for the school, give it a little class."

The idea of doing it with someone else was a lot more appealing than doing it alone. "You think Steve will mind?"

"Hell, no. He's always hinting around that I should get a job. It's just that most of the jobs I could get wouldn't even *pay* for a nursery school. This way I'd get free—I *would* get free tuition for any kids I might have, wouldn't I?"

Madelyn smiled. "Of course. And that goes for me, too. If I ever have any, that is."

"That's right, we did determine you weren't pregnant."

Madelyn laughed aloud. She couldn't remember now why she had ever thought Suzanna was snotty. She was nice and bright and funny, and Madelyn had the feeling they'd work very well together.

"I guess I'd better go. I stop in and see Babba every day."

"Better warn her you might not be doing that in the future."

"Maybe Eddie . . ."

"Hey, you're going to see him again. And the best thing for your relationship is if you're as busy as he is."

"I guess so."

"I never could figure out why you kept living off your folks. I mean, I know they have the money, but you were always so intelligent, I figured you'd want to do something."

"Every time I tried, they always made fun of my job. They thought any job I ever considered was always 'demeaning,' the kind of job other girls had, but not their daughter."

"Yeah, I could always see those two had you bull-dozed."

"They had my welfare at heart."

"Oh, sure, and you were pretty sick there for about a year, right?"

"I think they would have loved to have me just stay home and be an invalid the rest of my life."

"They'll all do that to you if you let them."

"Well, I let them. And every time I'd say something about how I'd like to pay my own rent, I'd get this lecture about how the buildings would one day be mine, and the tax structure, and how they were saving money by my not paying rent, and they'd finally wear me down and I'd just give in."

"My mom's not quite as strong as Aunt Shirley."

"*No* one's as strong as my mother. Or as stubborn as Babba. When I was a kid I used to think I must've been adopted."

"Every kid thinks that."

"You, too?"

"Everyone I know."

Not Eddie, thought Madelyn. *He had probably grown up wishing someone would adopt him.*

"If you want," said Suzanna, "I'll phone around and find out about licenses and stuff. And we can start reading the classifieds for a space."

"I'll find out about getting a loan."

"Come on by later this week and we'll have a business meeting."

What Madelyn was feeling was part elation and the rest anxiety. "You really think we can do it?"

"Why not?"

"We should've thought of this years ago."

"Years ago, honey, I didn't have a kid."

EDDIE CALLED her that night. It was about ten, about the time she had given up expecting to hear from him. She had been looking around her apartment and finding that everything reminded her of him. She was thinking she would rather move than stay there and be constantly reminded that for a few weeks she had been happier there than she had ever been. And that the source of that happiness had moved on.

"How are you, Madelyn?"

She didn't know how to answer that. He wouldn't want to hear an honest answer and she wasn't up to lying. "How's it working out for you, Eddie?"

"Good. Really good. I spent all day yesterday, and part of the night, with Bull, the guy I'm taking over for."

That was somewhat of an excuse, but he still could have called. He must have known she'd be anxious to hear from him. "What's the apartment like?"

"You'll have to come over and see it." But he didn't name a date or a time.

"Well, it sounds like everything's going well for you. When do you start school?"

"I'm not even accepted yet. But if I am, it starts in a couple of weeks. I did have some bad news, though."

"What's that?" She hoped it was bad enough to send him back to her, and then hated herself for hoping that.

"They're not accepting my correspondence courses for credit."

"What bad luck, Eddie."

"Yeah. What it means is, I'll be starting off as a freshman."

"Four years?"

"If I go summers, I can do it in three."

"That's a long time."

"I know."

"Three years," she said, thinking she'd be thirty-four by the time he graduated.

"I guess I'm lucky, though. It would have taken me that long anyway at another school, maybe even longer, because I would have had to work just to pay to go to school. I can go full-time with this job."

"I guess I hadn't really thought about it."

"Madelyn, the time'll go fast."

For him maybe, not for her. "I had lunch with Suzanna today," she said hoping he would tell her what he had done.

"Well, listen, I've got to hang up now. One of the women in the building, one of the professors, is paying me to walk her dog at night for her. I'm going to take it around the park once; that ought to do it. I'm going to take it out at noon for her, too."

"You're near the park?"

"Oh, yeah—you don't even know where I live, do you? Right across from Washington Square Park. I don't have a view, of course, but I like this neighborhood."

He should, it was one of the best in the city. "I'm glad you called, Eddie, I was wondering how you were doing."

"To tell you the truth, I meant to call you last night but Bull and I were out drinking beer and I had a few too many."

She felt her mood lighten. "I miss you," she said. She didn't know whether it was a smart thing to say, but it was what she felt.

"I miss you, too. Why don't you come by tomorrow, see my place?"

"I'd like to."

He gave her his address and then he told her he loved her, and she said she was glad, and then they said good-night, and when she hung up she wasn't sure whether she felt better or not. The thing was, they had been so polite, almost like strangers. His voice even sounded different.

And then she realized they'd never had a long conversation on the phone before. She didn't think she liked talking to him on the phone. She wanted him there in person, wanted to be able to watch the expression on his face when he said something. Talking on the phone wasn't even as satisfactory as writing letters.

She went to the kitchen cupboard and got down the files of his letters. It was time to get rid of them. They had long ago moved on to a new phase in their relationship. And no matter what happened in the future, she didn't want to end up alone, reading his letters for company. She wanted him or nothing at all.

As long as she was filling her trash can with letters, she also threw out the clippings. She had better things to dream about now than robbing banks.

She had her business to start planning.

Chapter Twelve

He'd told her he wanted to start from the beginning, do things right, go out on dates like normal couples. Only now he couldn't even afford to take her out on a date. At least not the kind of date he'd like to take her on.

Walking Professor Frank's dog had been a bonus. He had been putting out the trash barrels when this small, older woman with a birdlike face had come up to him on the sidewalk and introduced herself. She told him that she had paid Bull twenty dollars a week to walk her dog at noon every weekday and at night, seven nights a week.

"I'm small," she explained to him, although he could see that for himself. "I've been mugged once while walking my dog around the park, and I don't plan on being mugged again. Also, I found it was much more convenient not to have to rush home on my lunch hour to take him out. And I can sit around in my robe at night and not have to get fully dressed again to go outside."

Eddie told her he'd be glad to take over walking the dog, and then, without even checking him out, she handed him a key to her apartment. Just for the noon walks, she told him; at night she was always at home.

An extra twenty a week would be the difference between eating and barely subsisting, and he felt like doing a dance right there on the sidewalk he felt so good. And if Bull had picked up extra money walking dogs, there might have been other ways he had, too. Ways he'd find out about as he went along.

Then, later that morning, he was cleaning up the lobby when one of the other tenants was returning to the building with a mess of luggage, and he helped her carry it all up to her apartment. When she handed him two dollars, he told her he couldn't take that.

"Don't be ridiculous. Bull would have stood around *waiting* for it," she told him. "Anyway, all of us in the building are aware the supers we get are students. I'm sure you can use the money."

So he had thanked her and pocketed it and then had wondered if he should hang around the lobby until Madelyn got there and maybe get lucky again. So he tried it for a while, but when no one else needed suitcases carried in, he went back to his apartment.

Madelyn arrived early, but that was all right because he wasn't doing anything but waiting for her. As soon as he opened the door to her, he kissed her. He figured things were strange enough without suddenly acting like she was some guest he didn't even know.

And then he saw the look on her face as she glanced around his apartment. She looked pretty impressed.

"Not bad, is it?" he said.

"Not bad! Eddie, this is *fantastic*. You get this whole place for nothing?"

He nodded, somehow feeling proud, as though he now had something of his own to brag about. He guessed that that moment was the first one where he really felt like a straight person, like an ordinary citizen. "It even came furnished."

"This could really be fixed up nicely."

"Well, that'll have to wait. I'm not sure when I get paid yet, and even then it's not going to run to more than basic necessities."

She turned worried eyes to him. "You need some money, Eddie?"

"No, Madelyn, I'm fine." About the last thing he wanted was to have to take anything more from her.

"I could loan you some if you needed it."

"Look, I'll be honest with you; I don't have enough to take you out to some fancy restaurant, like I'd like to do, but I'm okay."

"We're friends, aren't we, Eddie?"

"You're my best friend."

"Then don't be too proud, okay? I mean, if there's ever some emergency, or you need a little loan until payday, please ask me. If you can't borrow money from friends, who can you borrow from?"

"Okay, but I'm making out all right."

"Promise, though?"

"I promise."

She was looking in at the kitchen now and shaking her head. "I can't believe how great this is. Even a separate kitchen. I wish I had that kind of cupboard space."

She walked into the bedroom and was back out in a few seconds. "You need sheets, Eddie?"

"No problem. I'll get some soon."

"You mean you won't even let me give you some sheets?"

"You've given me enough, Madelyn."

"Eddie, I'm just talking about those sheets you used on the couch. I don't need them. I'm not going to have anyone else sleeping on my couch."

He decided he was being so independent it was bordering on boorishness. "Thanks. I'd appreciate that. But you'll get 'em back when I get some of my own. Beggars can't be choosers, but I'd really prefer ones without pink flowers all over them."

Madelyn smiled. "Come on, Eddie, you always looked adorable in those sheets."

"Adorable? You're calling me adorable?"

"I can remember some very pleasant times on those sheets."

So could he. He had been keeping his distance from her in the apartment, not even following her into the bedroom, because he would hate to have her get the idea that he missed the sex as much as he did. Or that that was the only thing he missed about her. But now, taking his cue from her, he said, "I imagine it's possible to have a good time even without sheets."

She was leaning against the wall, smiling at him. "You really think that's possible?"

"Well, we could conduct a little experiment, kind of like gathering scientific data."

She moved away from the wall and began unbuttoning her coat. "That might be interesting. Just as an experiment, of course."

He folded his arms across his chest. "But then again, you might prefer waiting until I get the flowered sheets."

"You playing games with me, Eddie?"

"Yeah."

She walked over to him and took his hand. "Let's move the game playing to the bedroom."

SHE TOLD HIM she was having dinner with her parents that night, but if he was going to be home, she'd bring by the sheets on the way to their place.

He said he'd be home. Then she left and the apartment began to seem very empty and very quiet. He didn't have a TV, he didn't even have a radio. He had nothing to read, not even a game to play. After looking through the entire apartment he saw that the only thing he did have was some cleanser and a sponge, so he went around the place giving it a good cleaning. He wasn't that big on cleaning, but it was something to do.

He was just heating up some soup when Madelyn came back. She was carrying two shopping bags and he began to protest when she brought out a couple of houseplants, but she said, "Come on, Eddie, it's only a housewarming gift. I'd do the same for any friend."

She said he couldn't put them on his windowsills because the radiators were right under the windows and the heat would kill the plants. Instead, she set one on each end table, where they'd still get some light, then took the sheets into the bedroom.

"You don't need to make my bed," he told her.

She was already coming back out of the bedroom. "I wasn't going to. I'm sure you learned how to make a bed in prison. You're probably better at it than I am."

He figured she'd say why she was having dinner with her folks, but she didn't and he decided not to ask. If she wanted him to know, she'd tell him, wouldn't she?

He had been hoping she'd say she'd come back after the dinner, maybe spend the night with him, but she didn't even hint around about it. The first night in his apartment he couldn't remember because he had passed out, but last night had been lonely. It seemed that in just a short time he had got used to having her in bed with him, got used to eating breakfast with her.

She still had her coat on, so she obviously wasn't staying. She walked over to him and reached into her purse, and for a minute he thought she was going to try to give him money, but instead, she handed him the old deck of cards. "I thought maybe you could use them. I've got the new deck."

"Yeah, thanks."

And then she was gone, and he realized his soup was boiling and probably he had ruined it. But at least he had something to do that night. He could play solitaire.

That sounded like a lonely kind of thing to do, but it wasn't as though it would last forever. Pretty soon he'd be in school and have studying to do and he'd probably wish he had some time to play solitaire.

Plus he had the dog to walk later on. Yeah, all in all, it was going to be a really exciting night in the big city.

MADELYN WAITED until after everyone had finished dessert—some kind of Russian pudding her mother had whipped up—to bring up the subject of the nursery school. Then she did so rather casually, as if it weren't the foremost thing on her mind.

She said, "Suzanna and I are thinking of opening a nursery school." She thought she knew what their reaction would be. When she had wanted to be a secretary one time, her mother had said, "Oh, Madelyn, your father and I both have secretaries," in the same tone of voice she would have used if Madelyn had said she was going to be a cleaning woman. Shirley would have said, "Oh, Madelyn, but we have a cleaning woman." Her parents both looked down on those kinds of jobs for their daughter.

"You want to be an entrepreneur, is that it?" asked her father, not sounding at all dismayed by the news.

"Well, I like children, and Suzanna has been trying to get Brian into a school and says they all have waiting lists. I also think it's about time I started supporting myself."

She expected her mother to jump in immediately at that and say nonsense, that there was no reason for her to support herself, but instead, Shirley said, "I think that's very enterprising of you. You found a demand and are going to create the supply."

"Were you going to do this at home?" asked her father.

"No, of course not, I barely have room for myself. Anyway, I think we'll need a space with either a yard or access to a park. Children need to be outdoors in good weather."

She saw her parents exchange looks, then Shirley said, "The place on Barrow Street," and her father said, "Just what I was thinking," and Madelyn said, "What's on Barrow Street?"

Her mother got a pleased expression on her face. "We own a brownstone over there and the first floor was just vacated. And it has a yard. A good-sized yard, if I'm not mistaken."

"Good-sized," agreed her father.

"What's the rent on it?" asked Madelyn, although Barrow, being the west part of the Village, had to be high.

"Around two thousand, I believe," said Shirley. "I'd have to look it up."

"Could Suzanna and I see it?"

Shirley was nodding. "I'll give you the key and you can go over on your own. How were you planning on financing this enterprise?"

"I was going to ask if you'd cosign a loan for me."

Her father was looking doubtful. "Of course we would, honey, but I doubt you'll get one. What do you think, Shirl?"

Her mother was nodding. "Why don't we just loan you the money?"

"I've taken enough from you," said Madelyn, wondering when she had started to sound like Eddie.

"Oh, we'd charge the same interest rate."

"Or we could invest in the business and take a percentage of the profits," suggested her father.

"No," said Madelyn, "I think I'd rather it was a loan."

Then her father said that maybe it would be so successful she could sell franchises later on, and her mother was getting into it and talking about improvements to be made on the building, and Madelyn realized it was the first time they had ever really listened to her, treated her as an equal. It was a heady feeling.

"How many bedrooms does it have?" she asked, thinking she could move out of her studio and live in the nursery school.

"I think it has three," her mother said, "and the living room is a good size for a playroom. The yard has some nice trees, and you'd have plenty of room for a sandbox and playground equipment and wouldn't have to cart them all off to the park every day. None of the parks are safe these days for children, anyway."

"What about zoning?" her father asked her mother.

"I'd have to look into that. I don't think there will be a problem, though."

She had thought she would want to go home right after dinner, but she found the conversation so interesting she stayed late, then, when she got home, she called Suzanna. She woke her up, but Suzanna said it was all right.

"That sounds perfect," said Suzanna when she had been told about Barrow Street. "I was hoping closer to home, but that's a great neighborhood. You've got all those rich, creative people living around there who will definitely want their kids in nursery school."

"Do you think it'd be okay if I lived there?"

"Sure, that'd be even better. That way you can pay rent to the business and lower our overhead."

Madelyn had been thinking she could live there for nothing, but of course that wouldn't be fair. And the studio she was living in could be rented and she'd no longer feel obligated to her parents.

Suzanna said she would leave Brian with her mother the next day and they could go look at the place. "Steve thought it was a great idea. He's going to loan us half the money, but he's charging me interest—can you believe it?"

"So are my parents. They said we could write it off, though, so why not?"

She would have called Eddie then but she realized she didn't have his phone number and didn't know what it was listed under. She didn't know why she hadn't told him about her idea except she thought maybe it would fall through, and she wanted to wait until it was a sure thing.

She thought things were going to work out better than she had expected. She would be working all day, so she wouldn't miss Eddie when he was in school; then, at night, he could study and she could read, and it would be almost like it was before. On weekends she was sure he would want her to be with him at his place, which was fine with her.

She just wished he'd let her fix up his place, but he'd probably say why bother fixing up a place that belonged to NYU? Well, for all she knew, the nursery school might make enough money so that she'd be able to buy the entire building and live on one of the other floors and rent the third out.

Fantasizing about making that kind of money was every bit as interesting as fantasizing about robbing a bank. The only difference was, she wouldn't end up in Brazil.

MADELYN WAS SPENDING most of her time with Suzanna. At first Suzanna had said, "You're going to have to take care of a lot of this on your own. Mom will baby-sit occasionally, but she's got this bridge club and charities she works for, and I haven't found a reliable baby-sitter."

"Bring Brian along," Madelyn suggested.

"You don't mind?"

"Why should I mind? I'm crazy about him."

"I know you are, but I've never understood it."

"Suzanna, you've got a great kid. I just hope all the kids we take care of are as great."

So Suzanna bundled him up and he was not only well-behaved, he seemed to thrive on being carted from place to place. The first place they took him was to Barrow Street to look at the apartment.

The yard didn't look like much with the bare trees and the trash the former tenant had left, but it was deep, with a brick wall all around it, and they agreed it would do very well.

"We can get one of those jungle gyms," said Madelyn, remembering how she had liked to climb them when she was a kid.

"And swings. All kids like to be pushed on swings."

Madelyn said, "Mom said something about a sandbox, but I don't know whether we want them bringing sand inside, do we?"

"I don't."

"In the summer, though, we can get a wading pool."

"We can all go in it," Suzanna suggested.

"And a seesaw. Kids like those."

"I don't think so. Kids get hurt on those all the time. And that reminds me," said Suzanna. "Steve said something about insurance, in case a kid gets hurt. Says it'll cost."

Everything was going to cost, thought Madelyn. Still, they had put it all down on paper—fifteen kids at a hundred dollars a week per kid, and they figured they'd come out with a nice profit after costs.

The inside of the apartment was also perfect. The kitchen was too small to feed fifteen kids at the same time, but then neither of them had ever seen a New York kitchen that would. The living room and dining area, though, was big enough to hold two picnic tables where the children could eat as well as do activities such as fingerpainting. And two of the bedrooms would hold the child-size folding cots that were needed for naps, leaving the third bedroom for Madelyn's use.

"You're sure you're not going to mind living here?" Suzanna asked her.

"I don't mind. I figure I'll be too tired at night to do anything but go to bed, and weekends I can spend at Eddie's place."

"This carpeting will have to go. Too bad, it's pretty nice."

"Tile, right?"

"Or outdoor carpeting. Something we can clean easily."

"Later we ought to be able to afford a cleaning service," said Madelyn.

"Yeah, later, when we're rich."

They exchanged pleased smiles.

One day they took the subway downtown to get a business license and argued about what they were going to name the school during the ride.

Suzanna was still in favor of a French name, but Madelyn said, "I, for one, can't pronounce a word of French, which would make me hesitant to call up the school if I couldn't even pronounce the name. You can still teach the kids French, although I'd hate to have them all running around saying things I couldn't understand."

"You can learn along with them."

"I still like the Blanket Brigade. It's cute."

"It's so cute it makes me want to throw up. All right, Mad, I'll give up the French if you'll give up the cute. Why not just call it the Barrow Street Playschool."

"Yeah, I guess."

"But you're not thrilled."

"No, you're right, it's nice and straightforward. I can live without cute."

"Well, I'm glad to hear that, Mad. I'd hate to be partners with someone who insisted on everything being cute."

"You know something, Suzanna? Babba's right, you *are* snotty." Then she sat in shock over what she had said, but she finally stole a glance at Suzanna and saw that she was laughing so hard the tears were rolling down her face.

"You know something, Mad? There's hope for you yet. Stick with me, kid, and you'll lose that ladylike demeanor entirely."

EDDIE WOULD BE GLAD when school started. Not that he wasn't somewhat apprehensive about it. About all he could remember of school was either ditching it or getting into trouble when he went. He was pretty sure he had changed over the years, but it would be a real shock if he found himself in the classroom with an overpowering urge to throw spitballs at the teacher, or worse.

He couldn't complain about his job because it was easy and the tenants were really nice. He put out word to them that he was available for errands, and now, twice weekly, he did grocery shopping for two of them, and so picked up some extra money. If he didn't try to live extravagantly, he was sure he would get along all right financially. He had even picked up another dog to walk from one of the tenants in a neighboring building with whom he had struck up a conversation in the park when they were both walking dogs.

He was really missing Madelyn, though, and hoped that when school started he would be too busy to miss her. The day after the dinner with her parents, she had come over after visiting Babba and told him her plans to open a nursery school.

He couldn't believe the change in her. She was full of talk and plans, and he had never seen her so animated. He thought it was a great idea and was glad she wouldn't just be sitting home doing nothing, as he was sure that would eventually make her jealous of his going to school.

Still, the new semester hadn't started yet and until it did, he had a lot of time on his hands. Only now, Madelyn didn't. They would usually spend a couple of hours together in the evening, but then she would leave in order to get up early in the morning, and he was left either to stare at the walls or to play solitaire.

Eddie was really beginning to hate solitaire.

He did find the public library on Sixth Avenue and got a library card, but there were only so many books he felt like reading in a week.

He found out he got paid twice a month, and when he got his first paycheck, he thought the hell with the budget, he was going to call Madelyn up for their first real date.

He waited until she got home from seeing him that evening, then called her up.

"Hi, this is Eddie," he said, almost feeling nervous, which was ridiculous. It was not as if she'd turn him down or anything.

"What's the matter?"

"Nothing's the matter. What I was wondering was, would you like to go out Saturday night?"

There was a silence, then, "Are you asking me for a date?"

"Sounds like it, doesn't it?"

"Hold on a second and let me look at my calendar."

"Your calendar?"

She chuckled. "I was only kidding, Eddie. I'd love to go out with you."

"I thought maybe a dinner and movie, unless you'd rather do something else."

"That sounds lovely."

"And then maybe afterward you'll invite me up for a drink."

"Maybe."

"Maybe?"

"Well, it is a first date, Eddie. I don't usually invite men up on the first date."

"I hope you don't invite men up at all. Except me, that is."

"I'll probably be pretty tired, though. We're painting the place on Saturday."

"You need some help?"

"No, I don't want you to see it until we're all finished."

"Is Steve helping?"

"Yes."

"How come he can see it and not me?"

"Oh, Eddie—I hate asking you to give up your Saturday."

"Give it up? What else do I have to do? Anyway, I ought to learn how to do it in case anyone here needs an apartment painted."

"Well, if you really want to..."

"Damn right I do."

That didn't turn out to be such a good idea, because the date was lost in the shuffle when the four of them didn't finish painting until almost midnight. They'd had a good time, though, and Eddie really got to like Suzanna and Steve. Afterward, they all went out for pizza and beer, and they were so tired by the time they split up, Eddie wasn't even going to ask if he could come up when he took her home.

"You don't want to come up?" she asked him when he didn't go inside with her.

"I'm bushed, aren't you?"

"Not *that* bushed."

"You sure?"

"Come on up and I'll prove it."

As it turned out, he wasn't that bushed, either.

And the next day turned out pretty nice. He had forgotten how comfortable her place was, being fully furnished and all. He didn't even mind sitting around watching television all afternoon.

He was watching "Wide World of Sports" and she was reading the paper when she looked up and said, "You want my TV set, Eddie?"

"I can live without TV," he told her.

"You sure?"

"Of course I'm sure. I'll turn it off right now if you want."

"Maybe I'll store it with my folks, then."

"Store it? What're you talking about?"

"I'm not going to have room for all this stuff over there, Eddie. I'm taking my stereo because we'll be playing music for the kids, but we don't want them watching television."

"So put it in your bedroom."

"No. Believe me, kids can sniff out a TV set. Anyway, I'd rather read at night."

"Look, I'll be glad to store it for you. I got plenty of room."

"You really don't mind?"

"Why should I mind?"

"What about some of my other stuff?"

"Like what?"

"Books, kitchen stuff, some of my furniture."

"Sure, I got the room. Hey, you're not trying to fix up my apartment in a sneaky way, are you?"

"Eddie, I'm only going to have one small bedroom over there. All I'm going to need is a bed, which I'll have to buy, and my clothes. Everything else I'm going to have to either store or get rid of."

After that they gradually began to move stuff from her place to his. At first it seemed strange to see her things in his place when she wasn't even there. But now that her games were over there and the TV and there was enough stuff in the kitchen to actually cook, she came over more often and it was almost as if he were living with her. They even resumed playing Scrabble, but now he beat her most of the time because she was always talking about the nursery school instead of keeping her mind on the game.

"See?" he said to her one night. "It *is* working out."

"What's working out?"

"Each of us having our own place."

But instead of giving him an argument, as he was kind of hoping she would, she just said, "Yes, you're right."

That made him glad school was starting the following week, because he was the one getting jealous of her activities, which was something he hadn't counted on.

Chapter Thirteen

School started, and Eddie was glad he had taken Bull's advice and signed up for late-afternoon and evening classes. Particularly the evening classes.

The students who went full-time days were mostly regular college-age students, and he found he didn't have anything in common with them. They were away from home for the first time and taking advantage of their newfound freedom in ways they thought were daring, which to him seemed naive and almost innocent. They were of a generation who seemed primarily interested in drugs and rock, and only incidentally interested in getting a degree. Eddie found, when he talked to them, that they spoke what almost amounted to a foreign language.

He preferred the night students. They were older, most of them came directly to school from work, and they were more serious about their studies. Some of them were married, most of them were into some kind of relationship, and while he might go out with them after class for a quick beer, that's all it ever was, unlike the day students, who thronged the bars in the area at night and drank as if there were no classes to-morrow.

He had thought that, since he was older and was serious about learning, the freshman classes he was required to take wouldn't prove difficult for him, but he was wrong. He had never been a real student in any sense of the word. The one thing that helped was his having read a lot in prison, which got him used to doing the amount of reading that was now required. His concentration was pretty good, too; when others in his classes were constantly looking at their watches or out the window, he had no trouble paying atten-tion to the lectures and taking notes.

He was also used to studying on his own, so the homework assignments didn't bother him. What did bother him was the vast amount of knowledge the other students brought with them to class—a knowl-edge he didn't possess. The little amount of learning that had been required for him to get his high school equivalency diploma had in no way prepared him for the quality of education at a university like NYU.

He found that in order to keep up with his fellow students, he had to study twice as hard as they did. Days, between his chores, and the time between his classes and when he went to bed, were spent studying. Weekends, when he could also have used the time to study, he spent mostly with Madelyn.

His apartment now resembled a larger version of Madelyn's old studio. Most of her furniture was there. Her pictures were hung on the walls. He had her TV set, but no time to watch it. The games were all there, and one of the younger profs in the building, Ansel

Worth, now stopped by occasionally to challenge him to a game of Scrabble.

The apartment now had everything he needed and more. He was making enough money to get by, plus a little left over, which he was putting in the bank. The studies were hard, but he liked the challenge. He wasn't going to be an A student, but he thought he could pull down mostly B's and a few C's. And, when he got to his major in accounting, which was some time off, he knew he'd be able to keep up and even make A's. Accounting seemed to come easily to him.

The only thing that wasn't going well was his relationship with Madelyn. They didn't fight—it wasn't that—and they were both still as much in love as ever, but there just didn't seem to be enough time for them to see each other, and he found he was lonely living alone.

Sure, it was nice to be independent, self-sufficient. It was nice not to have to be living with a bunch of people he didn't give a damn about and with someone in authority always looking over his shoulder. It was even nice to have a little privacy, which had never been possible in Madelyn's one room. But it was nowhere near as nice—didn't even come close to being as nice—as living with her had been.

He figured she'd be hinting to move in with him, but she never did. If she had, he was ready at this point to give in. Where before he had only been concerned with not living off her and with living alone for the first time in his life, now he could see definite advantages to living with her.

For one thing, he couldn't see a whole lot of point to two people who loved each other living separately. For another, it was the only way he could think of where they'd have some time together. Sure, she'd be working all day, but he needed that time to do his job and get some studying in, anyway. And at night it would sure be nice to come home to someone, maybe talk to her about how school was going and listen to her tell him about the nursery school. And sure, he'd still have some studying to do, but he could do that in the bedroom and she could watch TV or read a book or do whatever she wanted.

Best of all, they'd be able to sleep together. And it wasn't just the sex, either, because they still had sex on the weekends when neither of them was worn out, and there wasn't a *damn* thing wrong with the sex. It was just that he had got used to having her in bed with him, and it had been the best thing he had ever known. The most intimate. In a way it was even better than sex, just knowing that she was beside him while he slept, would be there when he woke up.

He almost wished she had never opened the damn nursery school. Sure, he liked seeing her become independent of her parents, and he was proud of what she had done. But now, the fear he had previously had that she would become too dependent on him and he wouldn't have the time for her, had instead become the other way around. Now she had something that occupied all of her thoughts and most of her time, and he was feeling left out. He supposed she had spoiled him when he had been living with her, but he had liked being spoiled.

One thing he'd done, he had taken over for her with Babba. When Madelyn could no longer visit her grandmother every day to do errands for her, when she could only get away maybe once a week—and even that was really putting the burden on Suzanna—Eddie had taken to stopping by Babba's place and helping out. He still found her entertaining as hell, but he also began to realize that Babba had never cared who it was who did things for her, as long as someone did them.

Eddie knew how much Madelyn loved her grandmother, but he was beginning to see that Babba was only concerned with herself. Oh, she liked Madelyn well enough, but she liked Eddie just as much, and that didn't seem right to him. He had tried to talk to Babba once or twice about Madelyn, but Babba was never interested. Babba lived in a world of her own, and other people never penetrated beyond the outer edges.

So he was lonely some of the time; he guessed he could live with that. Judging by the hundreds of personal ads in the newspapers, it was a common condition in the city. Yet it was different with him. He wasn't lonely for other people; he was just lonely for Madelyn most of the time. And even the weather was conspiring to keep them apart.

January was getting all the snow Madelyn had hoped to see in December. He loved the way it made the city look and especially Washington Square Park, and it did keep him busy shoveling the sidewalk in front of the building. But it also prevented them from spending Saturday night and Sunday together for two weekends in a row.

They were the first two full-fledged blizzards of the season, both falling on weekends, and when they talked on the phone and he said he'd go to her place, she told him not to even bother. The streets over there hadn't been cleared yet. So they talked for a long time on the phone, but by the second weekend it meant that they hadn't been together in three weeks.

The second Sunday, thinking anything was better than not seeing her, he started off early, and what should have been about a twenty-minute walk took him almost two hours. And then, when he got there, she wasn't home. As it turned out, she had got up early and walked to his place, and when he wasn't home, she had gone to a bookstore and then to a movie matinee. If he had taken Christopher Street they probably would have run into each other, but he had gone a different way.

And sure, it was funny later when they exchanged stories, but at the time it had been frustrating as hell. In fact, he was beginning to realize how it must have been for the other convicts who had wives or girlfriends on the outside. If you didn't have someone it wasn't as bad. But when you did have someone you loved, and then you couldn't see that someone, it was pure hell.

And winter was just starting. The way it was going, it might be spring before he saw Madelyn again.

MADELYN ADORED the Barrow Street Playschool. She thought that she and Suzanna had created the most marvelous nursery school that had ever been in existence.

Everything about its physical appearance pleased her. She loved the child-size wooden furniture in primary colors. She adored the colorful posters depicting children from other lands in their native costumes, which they had purchased at UNICEF and had framed to cover the walls. Even the folding cots with their blankets of red, green, yellow and blue pleased her. And the yard, with the playground equipment, was a constant source of delight.

The immediate success of the school had been amazing. It had only taken one ad in the *Village Voice* for them to get all the children they were allowed by law to take, and then they had their own waiting list. They even had people begging to work for them, and one young mother—whom they both had taken a liking to, but who couldn't really afford the charge since she didn't work—they hired to help out three days a week in exchange for three days of nursery school for her daughter.

Except for two hours in the afternoon when the children napped, they were kept busier all day than either of them had ever been. Suzanna taught the children games and songs in French and even some elementary piano on the old upright they had bought and painted bright yellow. She was also the one who prepared the lunches and snacks.

Madelyn took over at other times with fingerpainting and crafts and would conduct a story hour twice a day, one to get them in the mood for naps and later to get them settled down and quiet before their parents came to pick them up. They both supervised the play-ground, but unfortunately, they were getting so much snow they didn't keep the children out long, since the kids seemed capable of soaking themselves through in a matter of minutes. They were both looking forward to warm weather.

They had mostly three- to five-year-olds, with a couple of two-year-olds who had been toilet-trained. There were no real troublemakers among the group, although one little girl, Tanya, would make a pest of herself tickling the other children if she wasn't watched. It wasn't that Madelyn or Suzanna objected to tickling per se; it was just that it nearly always re-sulted in the one being tickled wetting his or her pants, and there were enough accidents of that kind without asking for more.

Madelyn and Suzanna figured out that in less than a year they would have paid off both Madelyn's par-ents and Steve, and at that time they planned on doing one of two things. They would either expand the nursery school or set up another branch. Suzanna was in favor of setting up a second school closer to where she lived. If that happened, they would each hire two helpers and then just run the schools themselves.

As far as Madelyn was concerned, there was only one drawback to the business, and that was living on the premises. It had seemed like a good idea at first, but what it actually amounted to was that her work was never done.

Since she lived there anyway, and since Suzanna had to go home during the rush hour and then cook din-ner for Steve, Madelyn insisted on doing the cleaning up herself. But little children can make very big messes, and she seldom finished in under two hours.

Another drawback was the telephone. Since the parents knew Madelyn lived in the school, they were constantly calling her at night to discuss their children. And since Madelyn was every bit as interested in the children as they were, she found that most of her own time was now school time.

While the apartment delighted her as a nursery school, little tables and chairs weren't all that comfortable to eat her own dinner on. Nor was fingerpainting something she wished to amuse herself with at night. She began to envy Eddie living with all her furniture and her TV and having that big, one-bedroom apartment all to himself.

Furthermore, they could have used the third bedroom as an office. They already had the telephone in there on a desk, with a file cabinet beside it, and all she had to herself was a single bed and a chest of drawers. They could have used the single bed for the occasional child who became ill and whom they wished to keep separate from the other children.

What would have been ideal would be to move in with Eddie. The disadvantages of living in the nursery school far outweighed the one advantage of not having to commute to her job. She'd be delighted to commute to her job, especially since that would mean she could be separated from that job after working hours.

She missed Eddie. She didn't miss him as much as she knew she would've missed him if she didn't have the school. She sometimes thought if she hadn't opened the business with Suzanna she would now be a virtual recluse, just staying at home and waiting for the moments when Eddie had the time to see her. Still, the free time she did manage to have was spent, to some degree, in missing him.

Eddie was doing just fine without her. He was busy with school, busy being a super, and she was proud of how far he had come since the day he had shown up at her apartment. He had developed a quiet self-confidence that was impressive; even Suzanna and Steve had remarked on it. He now moved with ease through the city streets and any phobias that were prison-related seemed to have vanished. And, along with the phobias, any dependency he had once had on her had also vanished. That was just as well. Despite having loved being his entire world for a short while, she didn't think she was strong enough to be someone's entire world forever. And, of course, that had gone both ways. She wouldn't have wanted Eddie to have that burden, either. Now that she was running her own business, she knew she would never again be content to go back to being the nothing kind of person she had been before.

But she missed him. Because of the snowstorms, three weeks had gone by with nothing but phone calls between them. Being around children all day was fun, but they didn't provide the kind of mental stimulation she got from Eddie. To say nothing of other kinds of stimulation. She and Suzanna had become close friends, but Suzanna went home to her husband at night. She missed being with a man, and the man she missed being with was Eddie.

It was Saturday morning, and even though no snow was being forecast for that weekend, she didn't want to take any chances. Forecasters were known to be wrong. Snow had been known to cancel out her dates with Eddie.

She wasn't going to take the chance of waiting until evening. She was going to go over there now. If he wasn't in, she would amuse herself looking in the shops on Eighth Street. If he was in, they would have two whole days and nights together, which still wouldn't make up for the last two weekends of total boredom. She had always thought being snowed in would be romantic; being snowed in alone, however, surrounded by children's toys without even a child to play with, was about as unromantic as she could imagine.

She already had some of her clothes over at his place, so all she took with her was a toothbrush and a book on child development she was reading.

She stopped at a bakery on the way and bought some raspberry-filled pastries that would go well with tea, stopped at a newsstand to get the morning *Times*, and arrived at his place a little before ten.

To find him not at home. That was all right, she had taken her chances. She walked back to Eighth Street and visited her favorite shoe stores, buying herself a pair of running shoes, which were the only shoes to wear when chasing children around, and two new pairs of leg warmers, which she had found were absolutely vital if she wanted to stand around the yard supervising the children and not end up with frostbitten legs.

She spent some time looking in the window of the pet store at a puppy so fat and furry it resembled a stuffed bear. In her mind she was trying to justify buying a dog for the nursery school and thinking how much the children would love it, but she couldn't justify saddling the puppy with so many small admirers who would probably make a nervous wreck of it in no time.

She had never been allowed a pet as a child, and later, her parents hadn't allowed pets in their buildings, and now it seemed as if suddenly it was what she wanted most in the world.

That was ridiculous. It was pure substitution for what she really wanted. A warm puppy beside her in bed would hardly compensate for not having Eddie in that same bed. And, while a dog might make it all right for her to talk to herself aloud, it couldn't carry on a conversation with her.

She finally managed to tear herself away from the store window and spent a little time in Dalton's on the other side of the street. She bought a paperback she thought Eddie would like, and also two new storybooks to read to the children. Both children's books, she realized as she left the store, had to do with puppies.

This time Eddie was home when she arrived. He looked surprised to see her, but he also looked pleased. And even though the pastries were stone-cold by then, he put them in the oven and heated them up and made a pot of tea.

"You in the neighborhood shopping?" he asked her, taking in her packages.

"If you want the truth, Eddie, I figured I better get over here before it started snowing."

"It's not supposed to snow this weekend."

"So they say, but I wasn't taking any chances."

He grinned. "Does that mean you missed me?"

"No, not at all. I love spending my weekends fingerpainting. I'm even getting good at modeling things in clay."

"You were the one who told me not to come over."

"Eddie, it was so bad people were deserting their cars in the street."

"I would've made it."

"Yes, and all I have is that small bed and a bunch of toys to play with."

"I can remember a certain night when you made us pretend to be children."

"That seems so long ago now, doesn't it?"

"A month isn't that long, Madelyn."

Maybe not, but it seemed like another life to her. She didn't want to say so, though; she didn't want to bring that time up, because if she did she knew she'd end saying something dumb, like how much she had loved living with him, when she knew how much he was enjoying living on his own for the first time. She could wait. Things were pretty good when she got to see him on weekends.

"I still haven't taken you out on a real date," he was saying.

"This is real. I'm not going anywhere."

"Yes, but I mean the kind where I pick you up."

. "Well, I'm not going all the way home, but you can walk out that door and come back and pretend you're picking me up here."

He chuckled. "The hell with real dates. I guess if I had really wanted that I would've dated when I was a kid. What do you want to do tonight?"

"Send out for some food and stay home and watch television."

"No movie or anything?"

"I would love to just sit around and relax."

That was, in fact, exactly what she had wanted to do, but later she wished she had opted for the movies. They had spent the afternoon playing Scrabble, then had sent out for Chinese food. Afterward, they were sitting on the couch holding hands, watching a movie, and Eddie said, "Listen, would you mind if I did some studying while you watched this? I've got an exam on Monday."

Of course she had to say it was perfectly all right, even though she was personally bored to death with the movie and had been thinking of turning it off so they could talk.

But that was just a small detail. That hadn't been what she really didn't like about the weekend. The thing she had hated was feeling like a houseguest. It was Eddie's apartment; so even though the kitchen was filled with her things, she didn't feel right about making herself at home and cooking up something if she felt like it. She was afraid if she did, Eddie would take it as a sign she was moving in on him, and she didn't want that.

All weekend she found herself asking his permission to take a shower, water his plants, clean up his kitchen. He hadn't been like that when he had lived with her, but she couldn't help herself. She had been brought up to be polite in someone else's house, and being polite meant asking permission for even the most basic things like using the bathroom, although she spared him that.

On Sunday, when he again said he had some studying he had to do, she decided to go home early, spend Sunday night at her own place. And since he didn't try to argue her out of it, she found herself once again feeling like a giant among the scaled-down nursery furniture, wishing for Monday to come quickly.

EDDIE CAME TO THE CONCLUSION that dating was a whole lot harder than living with someone.

The entire weekend he had felt that he had constantly to entertain Madelyn. He had even felt guilty on Saturday night when he had gone in the bedroom to study for a couple of hours, even though she had wanted to watch television in the first place.

If he had still been living at her place and he had wanted to study, it would have been different somehow. She would have had things to do, she could even have gone out if she wanted, but when you were sort of on a date, you didn't just go out for a while. At least he didn't think so.

And Madelyn had been so polite it had unnerved him. She didn't seem at ease in his apartment, even though it was filled with her things. She kept asking if she could do things, as though he didn't water the plants regularly or couldn't clean up his own kitchen.

The sex hadn't been all that good, either. He took the blame for that. He knew his mind was still on his exam, that he was distracted, but she could have pulled him out of that distraction if she had made the effort. And then, after they had made love and he felt like talking, she had been asleep before he could even form his thoughts.

He hadn't been surprised when she went home Sunday evening. He guessed he hadn't been that entertaining, in or out of bed.

Next time he would try to get ahead with his studying before he saw her, then take her out somewhere. But hell, he hadn't expected her to show up so early. If he had had all day Saturday to study, he wouldn't have had to do it when she was there.

At some point Eddie realized he had stopped comparing the outside to prison and was instead comparing living with Madelyn to living alone.

There was no comparison.

It would sure be a lot simpler if she'd just move in with him. Dating—it just didn't seem natural. Maybe for high school kids who weren't old enough to live together, but not for two adults.

Sometimes it seemed to him that prison was a whole lot simpler than life on the outside.

Chapter Fourteen

Madelyn was beginning to wonder if she had an obsessive personality. She had clearly been obsessed with writing to Eddie when he was in prison. She had bordered on obsessiveness with her bank robbery clippings and fantasies.

Now she was becoming obsessed with a puppy.

Three times in the week following her first glimpse of the furry ball, she had found herself back on Eighth Street, looking in the window. She told herself it recognized her by now, but of course that was ridiculous.

The fourth time, when she passed by the shop and the puppy was gone, she was so upset she just stood there, blocking the sidewalk. It wasn't until someone said, "Excuse me, lady," in a tone that conveyed it wasn't the first time it had been said, that she recovered and stepped into the doorway to the shop. It was just that she had begun to think of it as her dog, and now it was obviously someone else's.

There was a diffident-looking man behind the counter of the pet shop, and she said to him, "You had a puppy in the window. I don't know what kind, but he was black and white and had a lot of fur."

"She's in the back," he told her. "We like to change our windows every few days."

Her relief was overwhelming. "Oh, I thought you had sold him."

"Were you interested in her?"

"Not really. I just thought he was so cute. What kind of dog is he?"

"She's an Old English sheepdog."

"Oh, a female," Madelyn said, finally paying attention to the gender. To Madelyn, cats always seemed female and dogs male, even though she knew it wasn't really that way.

"Would you like to hold her?"

She wasn't going to fall for that. She was sure that many people were lured into buying pets once they had actually held them in their arms. "Do they get very big?"

"Quite large," said the man, then took out a book from under the counter and showed her a picture of a full-grown sheepdog.

Now that she saw the picture she knew she had seen dogs like that around the city. They were the kind of dogs she always felt like hugging. Unlike others, notably Dobermans, whom she always trod by carefully.

"A big dog like that, can you keep her in an apartment?"

"Oh, yes—next best thing to a sheep ranch."

"They don't need exercise?" she asked, thinking of a dog that size running wild in a small room.

"They're lazy dogs. A couple of walks a day usually suffice. Even if they have a big yard to run around in, they usually just find a corner and go to sleep."

"Are they good with children?"

"Gentle as lambs."

Unfortunately, the dog had passed all tests. Madelyn was hoping it would fail at least one, thus putting an end to her obsession.

Declining again to hold the dog, she left the store and bought two more new picturebooks about dogs instead.

The next day she said to Suzanna, "I wonder if Eddie gets lonely living alone."

"I imagine so," said Suzanna.

"Why do you say that?"

"Oh, you know men; they hate living alone. They don't manage nearly as well as women."

"Do you suppose that's why so many men have dogs?"

"Probably. I know Steve wanted a dog, but we had a baby instead."

"Oh, come on, Suzanna."

"I mean it. He was talking dogs and I was talking cats, then the next thing we knew I was pregnant, so we started talking babies."

That night, when she was on the phone with Eddie, she casually asked him if he had ever had a pet as a child.

"Not one of my own, no. One of the families I lived with had canaries. I used to want to let them out of their cages, give them their freedom, but the lady caught me opening one of the cages one day and gave me a beating.''

''She beat you just for that?''

''She loved those birds. She used to put the radio on and they'd sing along with it. Once a neighbor's cat got in the house—well, to tell the truth I let it in—and you should have heard the commotion. I got a beating that time, too.''

''You like cats?'' she asked him.

''I guess so. I've never had one.''

''You like the dogs you walk?''

''Sure. What're you getting at, Madelyn?''

''Nothing. I never had a pet, either. I was thinking maybe we ought to have pets at the nursery school, but Suzanna didn't think it was a good idea.''

''All those kids. That much affection might kill a pet.''

The conversation decided her. If she couldn't have the puppy, she'd get it for Eddie. He needed a pet. He needed a companion, something to love. And walking the dog wouldn't be any trouble for him because he could walk it when he walked the others.

Yes, it was definitely what Eddie needed. He must get lonely at times living alone, even though he never mentioned it. A dog would be company for him. She could picture them eating together, the dog curled up at his feet when he studied, Eddie taking the dog over to the park and teaching it to fetch sticks. It was exactly what Eddie needed.

She'd still be lonely, of course, but she'd be able to see the dog on weekends. It would be something they could share. It would be almost like having a child with Eddie.

The dog was costly, but Eddie didn't have to know that. It even came with papers. Later on, if he wanted to, Eddie could breed her, sell her puppies for some extra money. Of course, by then she hoped they'd be together. Despite how well Eddie was getting along on his own, she still believed they'd be together some-day.

In the meantime, the puppy would be a strong bond between them. And she already knew his building al-lowed pets.

She would stop by the pet store, put down a deposit on the dog, and the following Saturday she would take it over to Eddie.

She couldn't wait to see his face when he saw her.

MADELYN INSISTED on meeting him at his place Sat-urday night, even though he still thought he ought to pick her up.

"Don't be silly," she said, "you're only a couple of blocks from the movie. Anyway, it's freezing out. I'll just get a taxi and come over."

That was thoughtful of her, he was thinking, not knowing it was downright devious on her part. But he didn't find that out until she turned up at his door with a shopping bag in one hand and a puppy in the other.

She put the puppy down and Eddie squatted down to pet it, saying, "You got yourself a puppy. Cute lit-tle thing. What's its name?"

She moved past him to the kitchen. "I got her for *you*." And then, while he stood there with his mouth open, she began to unload the shopping bag. It contained two plastic feeding bowls, a collar and leash, and about a ton of dog food.

She had got him a *dog*? Is that what she said? Why would she get him a dog? "I don't think I heard you right, Madelyn."

She was beaming at him. "She's for you, Eddie. I figured you could use some company."

Dogs might be fine, but what he needed for company wasn't a dog. He needed Madelyn. Living alone sounded great in theory, but it wasn't anything near to how great it had been living with her. "So you got me a *dog*?"

"You said you never had a pet of your own."

He was beginning to feel annoyed. He had a feeling that now she was working, he wasn't so important to her anymore. "You said you didn't, either. Why don't *you* keep her?"

"Eddie, she's for you. I thought maybe you were lonely living alone. You don't have to be ashamed to admit you'd like some companionship."

He'd like some companionship all right, but it wasn't a dog he'd had in mind. What was she trying to do, substitute a puppy for herself?

"I don't want a dog, Madelyn."

"Oh, Eddie, you'll love her."

"I don't think you heard me," he said more loudly, getting angry now.

She looked at him, her eyes wide. "You don't want her?"

"That's right."

Lower lip trembling, she threw everything back in the shopping bag, then scooped up the puppy in one arm and headed for the door. He could tell he had hurt her, which hadn't been his intention.

"Where're you going?" he asked her.

"Obviously, we're not wanted here."

"All I said was I didn't want a dog. I didn't say you had to go."

She stood at the front door with her back to him. "I'm sorry, Eddie. I guess I thought because I get lonely living alone, you did, too. I was wrong. I apologize."

"You're lonely?" That was about the best news he had heard in a long time.

He saw her head nod.

Come on, Eddie, say it. Tell her how you feel. "Hell, Madelyn, it's not a dog I want, it's you."

She turned around slowly, the corners of her mouth turned down in that sad smile of hers. "You already have me."

"I mean here. With me. I don't like this dating business. I liked it the way it was before."

She was looking uncertain and he wondered if he should have exposed his feelings like that. "It can't be like it was before. I don't live there anymore," she said.

"You could move in here with me."

Madelyn put the shopping bag on the floor and let the puppy loose. The puppy made a puddle, but neither of them moved to clean it up. "I thought you wanted to live alone."

"Yeah, I did. But I got tired of it real quick. You spoiled me, Madelyn. You made me see how perfect things could be. This dating business—the kids can have it. I thought I had missed out on something, but what I'm really missing is what we had together."

"So why didn't you say something before?"

"I figured *you* would. When you didn't, I figured you were happy with the way things were."

With just a slight shifting of the lips, her mouth took on a stubborn look. "I'm not moving in without the dog."

He was starting to smile. "Listen, I'd love to have a dog. I don't mind a dog."

"I'll pay you the rent I'm paying over there."

"No, absolutely not. I don't pay any rent here, so I don't know why you should."

"You can't afford to support me, Eddie."

"What're you going to cost me, a little food? If it makes you happy, we can split the grocery bill."

She was relaxing now, leaning back against the door. "It'll sure be an improvement over feeling like a houseguest when I'm here."

"You felt like a guest?"

She shrugged. "It's your place."

"And I felt like I had to entertain you all the time."

"I would still expect to be entertained at times, Eddie," she said, but he could see she was referring to the kind of entertainment he would be glad to provide.

"Just one thing, Madelyn—one condition I have."

"I have to shovel the sidewalk, right?"

"You have to marry me."

He could see that had been a shocker, no smart comeback to that one. "I never had a family, Madelyn. I want us to be one. Legal and all. These days I want to do everything legal."

"There's no hurry, Eddie."

"You know what Babba said to me? She said you were just like her, that you'd probably always live alone, like she does."

"Oh, Eddie, I'm nothing like Babba."

"That's what I thought. So we'll get married, right?"

"Right," she said, smiling.

And then he was about to take her in his arms and kiss her, which is the way things like that were done, but the phone rang. He debated whether to answer it, decided it was part of his job and picked it up.

He listened for a minute, then turned to Madelyn. "It's Babba. She's in jail and wants us to bail her out."

"That's what I call perfect timing," said Madelyn.

"We'll do it, right?"

"You might as well learn how, now that you're going to be part of the family."

He liked the sound of that. "Hang in there, Babba. We'll be right over."

"Will it bother you?" she asked him after he had hung up. "Being in a jail again, I mean."

He reached for her and pulled her close. "As long as I've got you, Madelyn, nothing's ever going to bother me again."

Of course, at that point, he hadn't seen what the puppy's teeth had done to his textbook. He was too busy kissing Madelyn to notice.

Harlequin American Romance

COMING NEXT MONTH

#141 THE STRAIGHT GAME by Rebecca Flanders

E. J. Wiley looked at the man across her desk—one Colby James. He claimed to be an itinerant sailor and dockworker. Honoraria Fitzgerald called him her long-lost son and heir to her San Francisco fortune. E.J. didn't know who was right—she only knew he was her fantasy.

#142 WINTER MAGIC by Margaret St. George

Even as Teddi watched the icy flakes falling from the warmth of the ski lodge, her drying throat constricted her breathing. It had been six years since she'd seen her family and friends—and snow. But it wasn't until her eyes lit on the indomitable Grant Sterling that she knew returning to Vail was her greatest mistake.

#143 A FAMILY TO CHERISH by Cathy Gillen Thacker

More than anything Christy Shannon wanted this family. Orphaned and now widowed, she couldn't understand why her husband had run away and denied his relatives. Until she visited the Texas ranch and met his brother, Jake. Jake opened his home to Christy, but he swore she'd never uncover the shocking incident that was the brothers' secret.

#144 A CLASS ABOVE by Carolyn Thornton

Squawking roadside chickens, rundown pickups and circling buzzards. It wasn't exactly what she expected when she accepted the challenge of this hitchhiking contest. For risk was Tara Jefferson's middle name. But little did she know that when she hitched a ride with pilot Marcus Landry he'd be taking her on the adventure of a lifetime.

Can you keep a secret?

You can keep this one plus 4 free novels

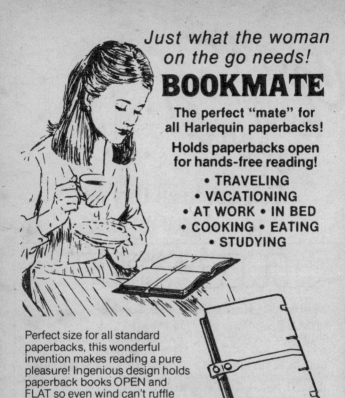

What the press says about Harlequin romance fiction...

"When it comes to romantic novels...
Harlequin is the indisputable king."
— *New York Times*

"...always with an upbeat, happy ending."
— *San Francisco Chronicle*

"Women have come to trust these
stories about contemporary people,
set in exciting foreign places."
— *Best Sellers*, New York

"The most popular reading matter of
American women today."
— *Detroit News*

"...a work of art."
— *Globe & Mail*, Toronto

WORLDWIDE LIBRARY IS YOUR TICKET TO ROMANCE, ADVENTURE AND EXCITEMENT

Experience it all in these big, bold Bestsellers— Yours exclusively from WORLDWIDE LIBRARY WHILE QUANTITIES LAST

To receive these Bestsellers, complete the order form, detach and send together with your check or money order (include 75¢ postage and handling), payable to WORLDWIDE LIBRARY, to:

In the U.S.
WORLDWIDE LIBRARY
901 Fuhrman Blvd.
Buffalo, N.Y.
14269

In Canada
WORLDWIDE LIBRARY
P.O. Box 2800, 5170 Yonge Street
Postal Station A, Willowdale, Ontario
M2N 6J3

Quant.	Title	Price
_____	**WILD CONCERTO**, Anne Mather	$2.95
_____	**A VIOLATION**, Charlotte Lamb	$3.50
_____	**SECRETS**, Sheila Holland	$3.50
_____	**SWEET MEMORIES**, LaVyrle Spencer	$3.50
_____	**FLORA**, Anne Weale	$3.50
_____	**SUMMER'S AWAKENING**, Anne Weale	$3.50
_____	**FINGER PRINTS**, Barbara Delinsky	$3.50
_____	**DREAMWEAVER**, Felicia Gallant/Rebecca Flanders	$3.50
_____	**EYE OF THE STORM**, Maura Seger	$3.50
_____	**HIDDEN IN THE FLAME**, Anne Mather	$3.50
_____	**ECHO OF THUNDER**, Maura Seger	$3.95
_____	**DREAM OF DARKNESS**, Jocelyn Haley	$3.95
	YOUR ORDER TOTAL	$_____
	New York residents add appropriate sales tax	$_____
	Postage and Handling	$___.7:
	I enclose	$_____

NAME _____

ADDRESS _____ APT.# _____

CITY _____

STATE/PROV. _____ ZIP/POSTAL CODE _____

WW-1-3